THE POT OF GOLD

AND OTHER STORIES

FLAX LOOKS INTO THE POT OF GOLD.

THE POT OF GOLD

AND OTHER STORIES

BY

MARY E. (WILKINS) FREEMAN

ILLUSTRATED

Short Story Index Reprint Series

BOOKS FOR LIBRARIES PRESS
FREEPORT, NEW YORK

First Published 1892
Reprinted 1970

STANDARD BOOK NUMBER:
8369-3390-7

LIBRARY OF CONGRESS CATALOG CARD NUMBER:
74-113661

PRINTED IN THE UNITED STATES OF AMERICA

CONTENTS.

LIST OF ILLUSTRATIONS.

LIST OF ILLUSTRATIONS.

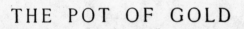

THE POT OF GOLD

THE POT OF GOLD.

THE POT OF GOLD.

THE Flower family lived in a little house in a broad grassy meadow, which sloped a few rods from their front door down to a gentle, silvery river. Right across the river rose a lovely dark green mountain, and when there was a rainbow, as there frequently was, nothing could have looked more enchanting than it did rising from the opposite bank of the stream with the wet, shadowy mountain for a background. All the Flower family would invariably run to their front windows and their door to see it.

The Flower family numbered nine: Father and Mother Flower and seven children. Father Flower was an unappreciated poet, Mother Flower was very much like all mothers, and the seven children were very sweet and interesting. Their first names all matched beautifully with their last name, and with their personal appearance. For instance, the oldest girl, who had soft blue eyes and flaxen curls, was called

Flax Flower ; the little boy, who came next, and had very red cheeks and loved to sleep late in the morning, was called Poppy Flower, and so on. This charming suitableness of their names was owing to Father Flower. He had a theory that a great deal of the misery and discord in the world comes from things not matching properly as they should ; and he thought there ought to be a certain correspondence between all things that were in juxtaposition to each other, just as there ought to be between the last two words of a couplet of poetry. But he found, very often, there was no correspondence at all, just as words in poetry do not always rhyme when they should. However, he did his best to remedy it. He saw that every one of his children's names were suitable and accorded with their personal characteristics ; and in his flower-garden — for he raised flowers for the market — only those of complementary colors were allowed to grow in adjoining beds, and, as often as possible, they rhymed in their names. But that was a more difficult matter to manage, and very few flowers were rhymed, or, if they were, none rhymed correctly. He had a bed of box next to one of phlox, and a trellis of woodbine grew next to one of eglantine, and a thicket of elder-blows was next to one of rose ; but he was forced to let his violets and honeysuckles and many others go entirely unrhymed — this disturbed him considerably, but he reflected that it was not his fault, but that of

the man who made the language and named the different flowers — he should have looked to it that those of
complementary colors had names to rhyme with each
other, then all would have been harmonious and as it
should have been.

Father Flower had chosen this way of earning his
livelihood when he realized that he was doomed to be
an unappreciated poet, because it suited so well with
his name; and if the flowers had only rhymed a little
better he would have been very well contented. As it
was, he never grumbled. He also saw to it that the
furniture in his little house and the cooking utensils
rhymed as nearly as possible, though that too was
oftentimes a difficult matter to bring about, and required a vast deal of thought and hard study. The
table always stood under the gable end of the roof, the
foot-stool always stood where it was cool, and the big
rocking-chair in a glare of sunlight; the lamp, too, he
kept down cellar where it was damp. But all these
were rather far-fetched, and sometimes quite inconvenient. Occasionally there would be an article that
he could not rhyme until he had spent years of thought
over it, and when he did it would disturb the comfort
of the family greatly. There was the spider. He
puzzled over that exceedingly, and when he rhymed it
at last, Mother Flower or one of the little girls had
always to take the spider beside her, when she sat
down, which was of course quite troublesome. The

kettle he rhymed first with nettle, and hung a bunch
of nettle over it, till all the children got dreadfully
stung.   Then he tried settle, and hung the kettle over
the settle.   But that was no place for it; they had to

go without their
tea, and every-
body who sat on
the settle bumped
his head against
the kettle.   At
last it occurred
to Father Flower
that if he should
make a slight
change in the lan-
guage the kettle
could rhyme with
the skillet, and sit
beside it on the
stove, as it ought,
leaving harmony
out of the ques-
tion, to do.   Ac-
cordingly all the
children were instructed to call the skillet a skettle,
and the kettle stood by its side on the stove ever
afterward.

The house was a very pretty one, although it was

quite rude and very simple. It was built of logs and had a thatched roof, which projected far out over the walls. But it was all overrun with the loveliest flowering vines imaginable, and, inside, nothing could have been more exquisitely neat and homelike ; although there was only one room and a little garret over it. All around the house were the flower-beds and the vine-trellises and the blooming shrubs, and they were always in the most beautiful order. Now, although all this was very pretty to see, and seemingly very simple to bring to pass, yet there was a vast deal of labor in it for some one; for flowers do not look so trim and thriving without tending, and houses do not look so spotlessly clean without constant care. All the Flower family worked hard; even the littlest children had their daily tasks set them. The oldest girl, especially, little Flax Flower, was kept busy from morning till night taking care of her younger brothers and sisters, and weeding flowers. But for all that she was a very happy little girl, as indeed were the whole family, as they did not mind working, and loved each other dearly.

Father Flower, to be sure, felt a little sad sometimes; for, although his lot in life was a pleasant one, it was not exactly what he would have chosen. Once in a while he had a great longing for something different. He confided a great many of his feelings to Flax Flower ; she was more like him than any of the other

children, and could understand him even better than
his wife, he thought.

One day, when there had been a heavy shower and
a beautiful rainbow, he and Flax were out in the garden tying up some rose-bushes, which the rain had
beaten down, and he said to her how he wished he
could find the Pot of Gold at the end of the rainbow.
Flax, if you will believe me, had never heard of it ; so
he had to tell her all about it, and also say a little
poem he had made about it to her.

The poem ran something in this way :

O what is it shineth so golden-clear
    At the rainbow's foot on the dark green hill?
'Tis the Pot of Gold, that for many a year
    Has shone, and is shining and dazzling still.
And whom is it for, O Pilgrim, pray ?
For thee, Sweetheart, should'st thou go that way

Flax listened with her soft blue eyes very wide open.
" I suppose if we should find that pot of gold it would
make us very rich, wouldn't it, father ? " said she.

" Yes," replied her father ; " we could then have a
grand house, and keep a gardener, and a maid to take
care of the children, and we should no longer have to
work so hard." He sighed as he spoke, and tears stood
in his gentle blue eyes, which were very much like
Flax's. " However, we shall never find it," he added.

" Why couldn't we run ever so fast when we saw the rainbow," inquired Flax, " and get the Pot of Gold ? "

" Don't be foolish, child! " said her father; " you could not possibly reach it before the rainbow was quite faded away ! "

" True," said Flax, but she fell to thinking as she tied up the dripping roses.

The next rainbow they had she eyed very closely, standing out on the front door-step in the rain, and she saw that one end of it seemed to touch the ground at the foot of a pine-tree on the side of the mountain, which was quite conspicuous amongst its fellows, it was so tall. The other end had nothing especial to mark it.

" I will try the end where the tall pine-tree is first," said Flax to herself, " because that will be the easiest to find — if the Pot of Gold isn't there I will try to find the other end."

A few days after that it was very hot and sultry, and at noon the thunder heads were piled high all around the horizon.

" I don't doubt but we shall have showers this afternoon," said Father Flower, when he came in from the garden for his dinner.

After the dinner-dishes were washed up, and the baby rocked to sleep, Flax came to her mother with a petition.

"Mother," said she, "won't you give me a holiday this afternoon?"

"Why, where do you want to go, Flax?" said her mother.

"I want to go over on the mountain and hunt for wild flowers," replied Flax.

"But I think it is going to rain, child, and you will get wet."

"That won't hurt me any, mother," said Flax, laughing.

"Well, I don't know as I care," said her mother, hesitatingly. "You have been a very good industrious girl, and deserve a little holiday. Only don't go so far that you cannot soon run home if a shower should come up."

So Flax curled her flaxen hair and tied it up with a blue ribbon, and put on her blue and white checked dress. By the time she was ready to go the clouds over in the northwest were piled up very high and black, and it was quite late in the afternoon. Very likely her mother would not have let her gone if she had been at home, but she had taken the baby, who had waked from his nap, and gone to call on her nearest neighbor, half a mile away. As for her father, he was busy in the garden, and all the other children were with him, and they did not notice Flax when she stole out of the front door. She crossed the river on a pretty arched stone bridge nearly opposite the house, and went directly into the woods on the side of the mountain.

Everything was very still and dark and solemn in the woods. They knew about the storm that was coming. Now and then Flax heard the leaves talking in queer little rustling voices. She inherited the ability to understand what they said from her father. They were talking to each other now in the words of her father's song. Very likely he had heard them saying it sometime, and that was how he happened to know it.

> " O what is it shineth so golden-clear
> At the rainbow's foot on the dark green hill ? "

Flax heard the maple leaves inquire. And the pine-leaves answered back :

> " 'Tis the Pot of Gold, that for many a year
> Has shone, and is shining and dazzling still."

Then the maple-leaves asked :

> " And whom is it for, O Pilgrim, pray ? "

And the pine-leaves answered :

> " For thee, Sweetheart, should'st thou go that way."

Flax did not exactly understand the sense of the last question and answer between maple and pine-leaves. But they kept on saying it over and over as she ran along. She was going straight to the tall pine-tree. She knew just where it was, for she had often been there. Now the rain-drops began to splash through the green boughs, and the thunder rolled along the sky. The leaves all tossed about in a strong wind and their soft rustles grew into a roar, and the branches and the whole tree caught it up and called out so loud as they writhed and twisted about that Flax was almost deafened, the words of the song :

" O what is it shineth so golden-clear ? "

Flax sped along through the wind and the rain and the thunder. She was very much afraid that she should not reach the tall pine which was quite a way distant before the sun shone out, and the rainbow came.

The sun was already breaking through the clouds when she came in sight of it, way up above her on a rock. The rain-drops on the trees began to shine like diamonds, and the words of the song rushed out from their midst, louder and sweeter :

" O what is it shineth so golden-clear ? "

Flax climbed for dear life. Red and green and golden rays were already falling thick around her, and at the foot of the pine-tree something was shining wonderfully clear and bright.

At last she reached it, and just at that instant the rainbow became a perfect one, and there at the foot of the wonderful arch of glory was the Pot of Gold. Flax could see it brighter than all the brightness of the rainbow. She sank down beside it and put her hand on it, then she closed her eyes and sat still, bathed in red and green and violet light — that, and the golden light from the Pot, made her blind and dizzy. As she sat there with her hand on the Pot of Gold at the foot of the rainbow, she could hear the leaves over her singing louder and louder, till the tones fairly rushed like a wind through her ears. But this time they only sang the last words of the song :

" And whom is it for, O Pilgrim, pray ?
For thee, Sweetheart, should'st thou go that way."

At last she ventured to open her eyes. The rainbow had faded almost entirely away, only a few tender rose and green shades were arching over her ; but the Pot of Gold under her hand was still there, and shining brighter than ever. All the pine needles with which the ground around it was thickly spread, were turned to needles of gold, and some stray couplets of leaves which were springing up through them were all gilded.

Flax bent over it trembling and lifted the lid off the pot. She expected, of course, to find it full of gold pieces that would buy the grand house and the gardener and the maid that her father had spoken about. But to her astonishment, when she had lifted the lid off and bent over the Pot to look into it, the first thing she saw was the face of her mother looking out of it at her. It was smaller of course, but just the same loving, kindly face she had left at home. Then, as she looked longer, she saw her father smiling gently up at her, then came Poppy and the baby and all the rest of her dear little brothers and sisters smiling up at her out of the golden gloom inside the Pot. At last she actually saw the garden and her father in it tying up the roses, and the pretty little vine-covered house, and, finally, she could see right into the dear little room where her mother sat with the baby in her lap, and all the others around her.

Flax jumped up. " I will run home," said she, " it is late, and I do want to see them all dreadfully."

So she left the Golden Pot shining all alone under the pine-tree, and ran home as fast as she could.

When she reached the house it was almost twilight, but her father was still in the garden. Every rose and lily had to be tied up after the shower, and he was but just finishing. He had the tin milk pan hung on him like a shield, because it rhymed with man. It certainly was a beautiful rhyme, but it was very inconvenient. Poor Mother Flower was at her wits' end to know what to do without it, and it was very awkward for Father Flower to work with it fastened to him.

Flax ran breathlessly into the garden, and threw her arms around her father's neck and kissed him. She bumped her nose against the milk pan, but she did not mind that; she was so glad to see him again. Somehow, she never remembered being so glad to see him as she was now since she had seen his face in the Pot of Gold.

"Dear father," cried she, "how glad I am to see you! I found the Pot of Gold at the end of the rainbow!"

Her father stared at her in amazement.

"Yes, I did, truly, father," said she. "But it was not full of gold, after all. You was in it, and mother and the children and the house and garden and — everything."

"You were mistaken, dear," said her father, looking at her with his gentle, sorrowful eyes. "You could not have found the true end of the rainbow, nor the true Pot of Gold — that is surely full of the most beautiful gold pieces, with an angel stamped on every one."

"But I did, father," persisted Flax.

"You had better go into your mother, Flax," said her father; "she will be anxious to see you. I know better than you about the Pot of Gold at the end of the rainbow."

So Flax went sorrowfully into the house. There was the tea-kettle singing beside the "skettle," which had some nice smelling soup in it, the table was laid for supper, and there sat her mother with the baby in her lap and the others all around her — just as they had looked in the Pot of Gold.

Flax had never been so glad to see them before — and if she didn't hug and kiss them all !

"I found the Pot of Gold at the end of the rainbow, mother," cried she, "and it was not full of gold, at all; but you and father and the children looked out of it at me, and I saw the house and garden and everything in it."

Her mother looked at her lovingly. "Yes, Flax dear," said she.

"But father said I was mistaken," said Flax, "and did not find it."

"Well, dear," said her mother, "your father is a poet, and very wise; we will say no more about it. You can sit down here and hold the baby now, while I make the tea."

Flax was perfectly ready to do that; and, as she sat there with her darling little baby brother crowing in her lap, and watched her pretty little brothers and sisters and her dear mother, she felt so happy that she did not care any longer whether she had found the true Pot of Gold at the end of the rainbow or not.

But, after all, do you know, I think her father was mistaken, and that she had.

THE COW WITH GOLDEN HORNS.

Once there was a farmer who had a very rare and valuable cow. There was not another like her in the whole kingdom. She was as white as the whitest lily you ever saw, and her horns, which curved very gracefully, were of gold.

She had a charming green meadow, with a silvery pool in the middle, to feed in. Almost all the grass was blue-eyed grass, too, and there were yellow lilies all over the pool.

The farmer's daughter, who was a milkmaid, used to tend the gold-horned cow. She was a very pretty girl. Her name was Drusilla. She had long flaxen hair, which hung down to her ankles in two smooth braids, tied with blue ribbons. She had blue eyes and pink cheeks, and she wore a blue petticoat, with garlands of rose-buds all over it, and a white dimity short gown, looped up with bunches of roses. Her hat was a straw flat, with a wreath of rose-buds around it, and she always carried a green willow branch in her hand to drive the cow with.

She used to sit on a bank near the silvery pool, and watch the gold-horned cow, and sing to herself all day from the time the dew was sparkling over the meadow in the morning, till it fell again at night. Then she would drive the cow gently home, with her green willow stick, milk her, and feed her, and put her into her stable, herself, for the night.

The farmer was feeble and old, so his daughter had to do all this. The gold-horned cow's stable was a sort of a " lean-to," built into the side of the cottage where Drusilla and her father lived. Its roof, as well as that of the cottage, was thatched and overgrown with moss, out of which had grown, in its turn, a little starry white flower, until the whole roof looked like a flower-bed. There were roses climbing over the walls of the cottage and stable, also, pink and white ones.

Drusilla used to keep the gold-horned cow's stable in exquisite order. Her trough to eat out of, was polished as clean as a lady's china tea-cup. She always had fresh straw, and her beautiful long tail was tied by a blue ribbon to a ring in the ceiling, in order to keep it nice.

The gold-horned cow's milk was better than any other's, as one would reasonably suppose it to have been. The cream used to be at least an inch thick, and so yellow ; and the milk itself had a peculiar and exquisite flavor — perhaps the best way to describe it, is to say it tasted as lilies smell. The gentry all about were eager to buy it, and willing to pay a good price for it. Drusilla used to go around to supply her cus-

DRUSILLA AND HER GOLD-HORNED COW.

tomers, nights and mornings, a bright, shining milk-pail in each hand, and one on her head. She had learned to carry herself so steadily in consequence that she walked like a queen.

Everybody admired Drusilla, and all the young shepherds and farmers made love to her, but she did not seem to care for any of them, but to prefer tending her gold-horned cow, and devoting herself to her old father — she was a very dutiful daughter.

Everything went prosperously with them for a long time; the cow thrived, and gave a great deal of milk, customers were plenty, they paid the rent for their cottage regularly, and Drusilla who was a beautiful spinner, had her linen chest filled to the brim with the finest linen.

At length, however, a great misfortune befell them. One morning — it was the day after a holiday — Drusilla, who had been up very late the night before dancing on the village green, felt very sleepy, as she sat watching the cow in the green meadow. So she just laid her flaxen head down amongst the blue-eyed grasses, and soon fell fast asleep.

When she woke up, the dew was all dried off, and the sun almost directly overhead. She rubbed her eyes, and looked about for the gold-horned cow. To her great alarm, she was nowhere to be seen. She jumped up, distractedly, and ran over the meadow, but the gold-horned cow was certainly not there. The bars were up, just as she had left them, and there was not a gap in the stone wall which extended around the meadow. How could she have gotten out? It was very mysterious!

Drusilla, when she found, certainly, that the gold-horned cow was gone, lost no time in wonderment and conjecture; she started forth to find her. "I will not tell father till I have searched a long time," said she to herself.

So, down the road she went, looking anxiously on either side. "If only I could come in sight of her, browsing in the clover, beside the wall," sighed she; but she did not.

After a while, she saw a great cloud of dust in the distance. It rolled nearer and nearer, and finally she saw the King on horseback, with a large party of nobles galloping after him. The King, who was quite an old man, had a very long, curling, white beard, and had his breast completely covered with orders and decorations. No convenient board fence on a circus day was ever more thoroughly covered with elephants and horses, and trapeze performers, than the breast of the King's black velvet coat with jeweled stars and ribbons. But even then, there was not room for all his store, so he had hit upon the ingenious expedient of covering a black silk umbrella with the remainder. He held it in a stately manner over his head now, and it presented a dazzling sight; for it was literally blazing with gems, and glittering ribbons fluttered from it on all sides.

When the King saw Drusilla courtesying by the side of the road, he drew rein so suddenly, that his horse reared back on its haunches, and all his nobles, who always made it a point to do exactly as the King did — it was court etiquette — also drew rein suddenly, and all their horses reared back on their haunches.

" What will you, pretty maiden?" asked the King graciously.

" Please, your Majesty," said Drusilla courtesying and blushing and looking prettier than ever, " have you seen my gold-horned cow ? "

" Pardy," said the King, for that was the proper thing for a King to say, you know, " I never saw a gold-horned cow in my life ! "

Then Drusilla told him about her loss, and the King gazed at her while she was talking, and admired her more and more.

You must know that it had always been a great cross to the King and his wife, the Queen, that they had never had any daughter. They had often thought of adopting one, but had never seen any one who exactly suited them. They wanted a full-grown Princess, because they had an alliance with the Prince of Egypt in view.

The King looked at Drusilla now, and thought her the most beautiful and stately maiden he had ever seen.

"What an appropriate Princess she would make!" thought he.

"Suppose I should find the gold-horned cow for you," said he to Drusilla, when she had finished her pitiful story, "would you consent to be adopted by the Queen and myself, and be a princess?"

Drusilla hesitated a moment. She thought of her dear old father and how desolate he would be without her. But then she thought how terribly distressed he would be at the loss of the gold-horned cow, and that if he had her back, she would be company for him, even if his daughter was away, and she finally gave her consent.

The King always had his Lord Chamberlain lead a white palfrey, with rich housings, by the bridle, in case they came across a suitable full-grown Princess in any of their journeys; and now he ordered him to be brought forward, and commanded a page to assist Drusilla to the saddle.

But she began to weep. "I want to go back to my father, until you have found the cow, your Majesty," said she.

"You may go and bid your father good-by," replied the King, peremptorily, "but then you must go immediately to the boarding school, where all the young ladies of the Court are educated. If you are going to be a Princess, it is high time you began to prepare. You will have to learn feather stitching, and rick-rack and Kensington stitch, and tatting, and point lace, and Japanese patchwork, and painting on china, and how to play variations on the piano, and — everything a Princess ought to know."

" But," said Drusilla timidly, " suppose — your Majesty shouldn't — find the cow " —

" Oh! I shall find the cow fast enough," replied the King carelessly. " Why, I shall have the whole Kingdom searched. I can't fail to find her." So the page assisted the milkmaid to the saddle, kneeling gracefully, and presenting his hand for her to place her foot in, and they galloped off toward the farmer's cottage.

The old man was greatly astonished to see his daughter come riding home in such splendid company, and when she explained matters to him, his distress, at first, knew no bounds. To lose both his dear daughter and his precious gold-horned cow, at one blow, seemed too much to bear. But the King promised to provide liberally for him during his daughter's absence, and spoke very confidently of his being able to find the cow. He also promised that Drusilla should return to him if the cow was not found in one year's time, and after a while the old man was pacified.

Drusilla put her arms around her father's neck and kissed him tenderly; then the page assisted her gracefully into the saddle, and she rode, sobbing, away.

After they had ridden about an hour, they came to a large, white building.

"O dear!" said the King, "the seminary is asleep! I was afraid of it!"

Then Drusilla saw that the building was like a great solid mass, with not a door or window visible.

"It is asleep," explained the King. "It is not a common house; a great professor designed it. It goes to sleep, and you can't see any doors or windows, and such work as it is to wake it up! But we may as well begin."

Then he gave a signal, and all the nobles shouted as loud as they possibly could, but the seminary still remained asleep.

"It's asleep most of the time!" growled the King. "They don't want the young ladies disturbed at their feather stitching and rick-rack, by anything going on outside. I wish I could shake it."

Then he gave the signal again, and all the nobles shouted together, as loud as they could possibly scream. Suddenly, doors and windows appeared all over the seminary, like so many opening eyes.

"There," cried the King, "the seminary has woke up, and I am glad of it!"

Then he ushered Drusilla in, and introduced her to the lady principal and the young ladies, and she was at once set to making daisies in Kensington stitch, for the King was very anxious for her education to begin at once.

So now, the milkmaid, instead of sitting, singing, in

a green meadow, watching her beautiful gold-horned cow, had to sit all day in a high-backed chair, her feet on a little foot-stool with an embroidered pussy cat on it, and do fancy work. The young ladies worked by electric light; for the seminary was asleep nearly all the time, and no sunlight could get in at the windows, for boards clapped down over them like so many eye-lids when the seminary began to doze.

Drusilla had left off her pretty blue petticoat and white short gown now, and was dressed in gold-flowered satin, with an immense train, which two pages bore for her when she walked. Her pretty hair was combed high and powdered, and she wore a comb of gold and pearls in it. She looked very lovely, but she also looked very sad. She could not help thinking, even in the midst of all this splendor, of her dear father, and her own home, and wishing to see them.

She was a very apt pupil. Her tatting collars were the admiration of the whole seminary, and she made herself a whole dress of rick-rack. She painted a charming umbrella stand for the King, and actually worked the gold-horned cow in Kensington stitch, on a blue satin tidy, for the Queen. It was so natural that she wept over it, herself, when it was finished; but the Queen was delighted, and put it on her best stuffed rocking-chair in her parlor, and would run and throw it back every time the King sat down there, for fear he would lean his head against it and soil it.

Drusilla also worked an elegant banner of old gold satin, with hollyhocks, for the King to carry at the head of his troops when he went to battle; also a hatband for the Prince of Egypt. This last was sent by a special courier with a large escort, and the Prince sent an exquisite shopping-bag of real alligator's skin to Drusilla in return. She was the envy of the whole seminary when it came.

The young ladies fared very delicately. Their one article of diet was peaches and cream. It was thought to improve their complexions. Once in a while, they went out to drive by moonlight; they were afraid of sunburn by day, and they wore white gauze veils, even in the moonlight, and they all had embroidered afghans of their own handiwork.

They used to sit around a large table over which hung a chandelier of the electric light, to work, and some young lady either played " Home, sweet Home, and variations," or else " The Maiden's Prayer," on the piano for their entertainment.

It seemed as if Drusilla ought to have been happy in a place like this; but although she was diligent and dutiful, she grieved all the time for her father.

Meantime, the King was keeping up an energetic search for the gold-horned cow. Every stable and pasture in the Kingdom was searched, spies were posted everywhere, but the King could not find her. She had disappeared as completely as if she had vanished altogether from the face of the earth. It at last began to be whispered about that there never had been any gold-horned cow, but that the whole had been a clever trick of Drusilla's, that she might become a Princess. An envious schoolmate, who had been very desirous of becoming Princess and marrying the Prince of Egypt herself, started the report; and it soon spread over the whole Kingdom. The King heard it and began to believe it; for he could not see why he failed to find the cow. It always exasperated the King dreadfully to fail in anything, and he never allowed that it was his own fault, if he could possibly help it.

At last the end of the year came, and still no signs of the gold-horned cow. Then the King became convinced that Drusilla had cheated him, that there never had been any such wonderful cow, and that she had used this trick in order to become a Princess. Of course, the King felt more comfortable to believe this, for it accounted satisfactorily for his own failure to find her, and it is extremely mortifying for a King to be unable to do anything he sets out to.

So Drusilla was dismissed from the seminary in disgrace, and sent home. Her jewels and fine clothes were all taken away from her, even her rick-rack dress, and she put on her blue petticoat and short gown, and straw flat again. Still, she was so happy at the prospect of seeing her dear old father again, that she did not mind the loss of all her fine things much. She did not ride the white palfrey now, but went home on foot, in the dewy morning, as fast as she could trip.

When she came in sight of the cottage, there was her father sitting in his old place at the window. When he saw his beloved daughter coming, he ran out to meet her as fast as he could hobble, and they tenderly embraced each other.

The King had provided liberally for the old man while Drusilla was in the seminary, but now that he was so angry at her alleged deception, his support would probably cease, and, since the gold-horned cow was lost, it was a question how they would live. The father and daughter sat talking it over after they had entered the cottage. It was a puzzling question, and Drusilla was weeping a little, when her father gave a joyful cry:

" Look, look, Drusilla!"

Drusilla looked up quickly, and there was the milk-white face and golden horns of the cow peering through the vines in the window. She was eating some of the pink and white roses.

Drusilla and her father hastened out with joyful exclamations, and there was the cow, sure enough. A couple of huge wicker baskets were slung across her broad back, and one was filled to the brim with gold coins, and the other with jewels, diamonds, pearls and rubies.

When Drusilla and her father saw them, they both threw their arms around the gold-horned cow's neck, and cried for joy. She turned her head and gazed at them a moment with her calm, gentle eyes; then she went on eating roses.

When the King heard of all this, he came with the Queen in a golden coach, to see Drusilla and her father. "I am convinced now of your truthfulness," he said majestically, when the Court Jeweler had examined the cow's horns to see if they were true gold, and not merely gilded, and he had seen with his own eyes the two baskets full of coins and jewels. " And, if you would like to be Princess, you can be, and also marry the Prince of Egypt."

But Drusilla threw her arms around her father's neck. " No; your Majesty," she said timidly, "I had rather stay with my father, if you please, than be a Princess, and I rather live here and tend my dear cow, than marry the Prince of Egypt."

The King sighed, and so did the Queen; they knew they never should find another such beautiful Princess. But, then, the King had not kept his part of the contract and found the gold-horned cow, and he could not compel her to be a Princess without breaking the royal word.

So the cow was again led out to pasture in the little meadow of blue-eyed grasses, and Drusilla, though she was very rich now, used to find no greater happiness than to sit on the banks of the silvery pool where the yellow lilies grew, and watch her.

They had their poor little cottage torn down and a grand castle built instead; but the roof of that was thatched and over-grown with moss, and pink and white roses clustered thickly around the walls. It was just as much like their old home as a castle can be like a cottage. The gold-horned cow had, also, a magnificent new stable. Her eating-trough was the finest moss rose-bud china, she had dried rose leaves instead of hay to eat, and there were real lace curtains at all the stable windows, and a lace *portière* over her stall.

The King and Queen used to visit Drusilla often; they gave her back her rick-rack dress, and grew very fond of her, though she would not be a Princess. Finally, however, they prevailed upon her to be made a countess. So she was called "Lady Drusilla," and she had a coat of arms, with the gold-horned cow rampant on it, put up over the great gate of the castle.

PRINCESS ROSETTA AND THE POP–CORN MAN.

I.

THE PRINCESS ROSETTA.

The Bee Festival was held on the sixteenth day of May; all the court went. The court-ladies wore green silk scarfs, long green floating plumes in their bonnets, and green satin petticoats embroidered with apple-blossoms. The court-gentlemen wore green velvet tunics with nose-gays in their buttonholes, and green silk hose. Their little pointed shoes were adorned with knots of flowers instead of buckles.

As for the King himself, he wore a thick wreath of cherry and peach-blossoms instead of his crown, and carried a white thorn-branch instead of his scepter. His green velvet robe was trimmed with a border of blue and white violets instead of ermine. The Queen wore a garland of violets around her golden head, and the hem of her gown was thickly sown with primroses.

But the little Princess Rosetta surpassed all the rest. Her little gown was completely woven of violets and other fine flowers. There was a very skillful

41

seamstress in the court who knew how to do this kind of work, although no one except the Princess Rosetta was allowed to wear a flower-cloth gown to the Bee Festival. She wore also a little white violet cap, and two of her nurses carried her between them in a little basket lined with rose and apple-leaves.

All the company, as they danced along, sang, or played on flutes, or rang little glass and silver bells. Nobody except the King and Queen rode. They rode cream-colored ponies, with silken ropes wound with flowers for bridle-reins.

The Bee Festival was held in a beautiful park a mile distant from the city. The young grass there was green and velvety, and spangled all over with fallen apple and cherry and peach and plum and pear-blossoms ; for the park was set with fruit-trees in even rows. The blue sky showed between the pink and white branches, and the air was very sweet and loud with the humming of bees. The trees were all full of bees. There was something peculiar about the bees of this country ; none of them had stings.

When the court reached the park, they all tinkled their bells in time, whistled on their flutes, and sang a song which they always sang on these occasions. Then they played games and enjoyed themselves. They played hide-and-seek among the trees, and formed rings and danced. The bees flew around them, and seemed to know them. The little Princess, lying in her basket, crowed and laughed, and caught at them when they came humming over her face. Her nurses stood around her, and waved great fans of peacock-feathers, but that did not frighten the bees at all.

The court's lunch was spread on a damask-cloth, in an open space between the trees. There were biscuits of wheaten flour, plates of honey-comb, and cream in tall glass ewers. That was the regulation lunch at the Bee Festival. The Bee Festival was nearly as old as the kingdom, and there was an ancient legend about it, which the Poet Laureate had put into an epic poem. The King had it in his royal library, printed in golden letters and bound in old gold plush.

Centuries ago, so the legend ran, in the days of the very first monarch of the royal family of which this king was a member, there were no bees at all in the kingdom. Not a child in the whole country, not even the little princes and princesses in the palace, had ever tasted a bit of bread and honey.

But, while there were no bees in this kingdom, one just across the river was swarming with them. That kingdom was governed by a king who was the tenth cousin of the first, and not very well disposed toward him. He had stationed lines of sentinels with ostrich-feather brooms on his bank of the river to keep the bees from flying over, and he would not export a single bee, nor one ounce of honey, although he had been offered immense sums.

However, the inhabitants of this second country were so cruel and tormenting in their dispositions, and the children so teased the bees, which were stingless and could not defend themselves, that they rebelled. They stopped making honey, and one day they swarmed, and flew in a body across the river in spite of the frantic waving of the ostrich-feather brooms.

The other King was overjoyed. He ordered beautiful hives to be built for them, and instituted a national festival in their honor, which ever since had been observed regularly on the sixteenth day of May.

Up to this day there were no bees in the kingdom across the river. Not one would return to where its ancestors had been so hardly treated ; here everybody was kind to them, and even paid them honor. The present King had established an order of the "Golden Bee." The Knights of the Golden Bee wore ribbons studded with golden bees on their breasts, and their watchword was a sort of a "buzz-z-z," like the humming of a bee. When they were in full regalia they wore also some curious wings made of gold wire and lace. The Knights of the Golden Bee comprised the finest nobles of the court.

In addition to them were the "Bee Guards." They were the King's own body-guards. Their uniform was white with green cuffs and collar and facings. On the green were swarms of embroidered bees. They carried a banner of green silk worked with bees and roses.

So the bee might fairly have been considered the national emblem of Romalia, for that was the name of the country. The first word which the children learned to spell in school was " b-e-e, bee," instead of " b-o-y, boy." The poorest citizen had a bush of roses and a bee-hive in his yard, and the people were very for-lorn who could not have a bit of honey-comb at least once a day. The court pre-ferred it to any other food. Indeed it was this particular Queen who was in the kitchen eating bread and honey, in the song.

But to return to the Bee Festival, on this especial six-teenth of May. At sunset when the bees flew back to their hives for the last time with their loads of honey, the court also went home.

A KNIGHT OF THE GOLDEN BEE.

They danced along in a splendid merry procession. The cream-colored ponies the King and Queen rode pranced lightly in advance, their slender hoofs keeping time to the flutes and the bells; and the gallants, leading the ladies by the tips of their dainty fingers, came after them with gay waltzing steps. The nurses who carried the Princess Rosetta held their heads high, and danced along as bravely as the others, waving their peacock-feather fans in their unoccupied hands. They bore the little Princess in her basket between them as lightly as a feather. Up and down she swung. When they first started she laughed and crowed; then she became very quiet. The nurses thought she was asleep. They had laid a little satin coverlet over her, and put a soft thick veil over her face, that the damp evening-air might not give her the croup. The Princess Rosetta was quite apt to have the croup.

The nurses cast a glance down at the veil and satin coverlet which were so motionless. " Her Royal Highness is asleep," they whispered to each other with nods. The nurses were handsome young women, and they wore white lace caps, and beautiful long darned lace aprons. They swung the Princess's basket along so easily that finally one of them remarked upon it.

" How very light her Royal Highness is," said she.

" She weighs absolutely nothing at all," replied the other nurse who was carrying the Princess, " absolutely nothing at all."

" Well, that is apt to be the case with such high-born infants," said the first nurse. And they all waved their fans again in time to the music.

When they reached the palace, the massive doors were thrown open, and the court passed in. The nurses bore the Princess Rosetta's basket up the grand marble stair, and carried it into the nursery.

"We will lift her Royal Highness out very carefully, and possibly we can put her to bed without waking her," said the Head-nurse.

But her Royal Highness's ladies-of-the-bed-chamber who were in waiting set up such screams of horror at her remark, that it was a wonder that the Princess did not awake directly.

"O-h!" cried a lady-of-the-bed-chamber, "put her Royal Highness to bed, in defiance of all etiquette, before the Prima Donna of the court has sung her lullaby! Preposterous! Lift her out without waking her, indeed! This nurse should be dismissed from the court!"

"O-h!" cried another lady, tossing her lovely head scornfully, and giving her silken train an indignant swish; "the idea of putting her Royal Highness to bed without the silver cup of posset, which I have here for her!"

"And without taking her rose-water bath!" cried another, who was dabbling her lily fingers in a little ivory bath filled with rose-water.

"And without being anointed with this Cream of Lilies!" cried one with a little ivory jar in her hand.

"And without having every single one of her golden ringlets dressed with this pomade scented with violets and almonds!" cried one with a round porcelain box.

" Or even having her curls brushed ! " cried a lady as if she were fainting, and she brandished an ivory hair-brush set with turquoises.

" I suppose," remarked a lady who was very tall and majestic in her carriage, " that this nurse would not object to her Royal Highness being put to bed without — her nightgown, even ! "

And she held out the Princess's little embroidered nightgown, and gazed at the Head-nurse with an awful air.

" I beg your pardon humbly, my Ladies," responded the Head-nurse meekly. Then she bent over the basket to lift out the Princess.

Every one stood listening for her Royal Highness's pitiful scream when she should awake. The lady with the cup of posset held it in readiness, and the ladies with the Cream of Lilies, the violet and almond pomade and the ivory hair-brush looked anxious to begin their duties. The Prima Donna stood with her song in hand, and the first court fiddler had his bow raised all ready to play the accompaniment for her. Writing a fresh lullaby for the Princess every day, and setting it to music, were among the regular duties of the Poet Laureate and the first musical composer of the court.

The Head-nurse with her eyes full of tears because of the reproaches she had received, reached down her arms and attempted to lift the Princess Rosetta —

suddenly she turned very white, and tossed aside the veil and the satin coverlet. Then she gave a loud scream, and fell down in a faint.

The ladies stared at one another.

" What is the matter with the Head-nurse?" they asked. Then the second nurse stepped up to the basket and reached down to clasp the Princess Rosetta. Then she gave a loud scream, and fell down in a faint.

The third nurse, trembling so she could scarcely stand, came next. After she had stooped over the basket, she also gave a loud scream and fainted. Then the fourth nurse stepped up, bent over the basket, and fainted. So all the Princess Rosetta's nurses lay fainting on the floor beside her basket.

It was contrary to the rules of etiquette for any one except the nurses to approach nearer than five yards to her Royal Highness before she was taken from her basket. So they crowded together at that distance and craned their necks.

" What can ail the nurses?" they whispered in terrified tones. They could not go near enough to the basket to see what the trouble was, and still it seemed very necessary that they should.

" I wish I had a telescope," said the lady with the hair-brush.

But there was none in the room, and it was contrary to the rules of etiquette for any person to leave it until the Princess was taken from the basket.

There seemed to be no proper way out of the difficulty. Finally the first fiddler stood up with an air of resolution, and began unwinding the green silk sash from his waist. It was eleven yards long. He doubled it, and launched it at the basket, like a lasso.

"There is nothing in the code of etiquette to pre-

THE PRINCESS WAS NOT IN THE BASKET!

vent the Princess approaching us before she is taken from her basket," he said bravely. All the ladies applauded.

He threw the lasso very successfully. It went quite around the basket. Then he drew it gently over the five yards.   They all crowded around, and looked into it.

The Princess was not in the basket !

II.

THE POP-CORN MAN.

That night the whole kingdom was in a turmoil. The Bee Guards were called out, and patrolled the city, alarm-bells rung, signal fires burned, and everybody was out with a lantern. They searched every inch of the road to the park where the Bee Festival had been held, for it did seem at first as if the Princess had possibly been spilled out of the basket, although the nurses were confident that it was not so. So they searched carefully, and the nurses were in the meantime placed in custody.   But nothing was found. The people held their lanterns low, and looked under every bush, and even poked aside the grasses, but they could not find the Princess on the road to the park.

Then a regular force of detectives was organized, and the search continued day after day.   Every house in the country was examined in every nook and corner.   The cupboards even were all ransacked, and the bureau drawers.   The King had a favorite book of philosophy, and one motto which he had learned in his youth recurred to him.   It was this:

"When a-seeking, seek in the unlikely places, as well as the likely ; for no man can tell the road that lost things may prefer."

So he ordered search to be made in unlikely as well as likely places, for the Princess ; and it was carried so far that the people had all to turn their pockets inside out, and shake their shawls and table-cloths. But it was all of no use. Six months went by, and the Princess Rosetta had not been found. The King and Queen were broken-hearted. The Queen wept all day long, and her tears fell into her honey, until it was no longer sweet, and she could not eat it. The King sat by himself and had no heart for anything.

But the four nurses were in nearly as much distress. Not only had they been very fond of the little Princess, and were grieving bitterly for her loss, but they had also a punishment to endure. They had been released from custody, because there was really no evidence against them, but in view of their possible carelessness, and in perpetual reminder of the loss of the Princess, a sentence had been passed upon them. They had been condemned to wear their bonnets the wrong way around, indoors and out, until the Princess should be found. So the poor nurses wept into the crowns of their bonnets. They had little peep-holes in the straw that they might see to get about, and they lifted up the capes in order to eat; but it was very trying. The nurses were all pretty young women too,

THE BEE GUARDS PATROLLED THE CITY.

and the Head-nurse who came of quite a distinguished family was to have been married soon. But how could she be a bride and wear a veil with her face in the crown of her bonnet?

The Head-nurse was quite clever, and she thought about the Princess's disappearance, until finally her thoughts took shape. One day she put on her shawl — her bonnet was always on — and set out to call on the Baron Greenleaf. The Baron was an old man who was said to be versed in white magic, and lived in a stone tower with his servants and his house-keeper.

When the Head-nurse came into the tower-yard, the dog began to bark; he was not used to seeing a woman with her face in the crown of her bonnet. He thought that her head must be on the wrong way, and that she was a monster, and had designs upon his master's property. So he barked and growled, and caught hold of her dress, and the Head-nurse screamed. The Baron himself came running downstairs, and opened the door. " Who is there? " cried he.

But when he saw the woman with her bonnet on wrong he knew at once that she must be one of the Princess's nurses. So he ordered off the dog, and ushered the nurse into the tower. He led her into his study, and asked her to sit down. " Now, madam, what can I do for you? " he inquired quite politely.

" Oh, my lord! " cried the Head-nurse in her muffled voice, " help me to find the Princess."

The Baron, who was a tall lean old man and wore a very large-figured dressing-gown trimmed with fur, frowned, and struck his fist down upon the table. " Help you to find the Princess ! " he exclaimed ; " don't you suppose I should find her on my own account if I could ? I should have found her long before this if the idiots had not broken all my bottles, and crystals, and retorts, and mirrors, and spilled all the magic fluids, so that I cannot practice any white magic at all. The idea of looking for a princess in a bottle — that comes of pinning one's faith upon philosophy ! "

" Then you cannot find the Princess by white magic ? " the Head-nurse asked timidly.

The Baron pounded the table again. " Of course I cannot," he replied, " with all my magical utensils smashed in the search for her."

The Head-nurse sighed pitifully.

" I suppose that you do not like to go about with your face in the crown of your bonnet ? " the Baron remarked in a harsh voice.

The Head-nurse replied sadly that she did not.

" It doesn't seem to me that I should mind it much," said the Baron.

The Head-nurse looked at his grim old face through the peep-holes in her bonnet-crown, and thought to herself that if she were no prettier than he, she should not mind much either, but she said nothing.

Suddenly there was a knock at the tower-door.

"Excuse me a moment," said the Baron; "my housekeeper is deaf, and my other servants have gone out." And he ran down the tower-stair, his dressing-gown sweeping after him.

Presently he returned, and there was a young man with him. This young man was as pretty as a girl, and he looked very young. His blue eyes were very sharp and bright, and he had rosy cheeks and fair curly hair. He was dressed very poorly, and around his shoulders were festooned strings of something that looked like fine white flowers, but it was in reality pop-corn. He carried a great basket of pop-corn, and bore a corn-popper over his shoulder.

When he entered he bowed low to the Head-nurse; her bonnet did not seem to surprise him at all. "Would you like to buy some of my nice pop-corn, madam?" he asked.

She curtesied. "Not to-day," she replied.

But in reality she did not know what pop-corn was. She had never seen any, and neither had the Baron. That indeed was the reason why he had admitted the man — he was curious to see what he was carrying. "Is it good to eat?" he inquired.

"Try it, my lord," answered the man. So the Baron put a pop-corn in his mouth and chewed it critically. "It is very good indeed," he declared.

The man passed the basket to the Head-nurse, and

she lifted the cape of her bonnet and put a pop-corn in her mouth, and nibbled it delicately. She also thought it very good.

"But there is no use in discussing new articles of food when the kingdom is under the cloud that it is at present, and my retorts and crystals all smashed," said the Baron.

"Why, what is the cloud, my lord?" inquired the Pop-corn man. Then the Baron told him the whole story.

"Of course it is necromancy," remarked the Pop-corn man thoughtfully, when the Baron had finished.

The Baron pounded on the table until it danced. "Necromancy!" he cried, "of course it's necromancy! Who but a necromancer could have made a child invisible, and stolen her away in the face and eyes of the whole court?"

"Have you any idea where she is?" ask the Pop-corn man.

The Baron stared at him in amazement.

"Idea where she is?" he repeated scornfully. "You are just of a piece with the idiots who broke my mirrors to see if the Princess was not behind them! How should we have any idea where she is if she is lost, pray?"

The Pop-corn man blushed, and looked frightened, but the Head-nurse spoke up quite bravely, although her voice was so muffled, and said that she really did have some idea of the Princess's whereabouts. She propounded her views which were quite plausible. It was her opinion that only an enemy of the King would have caused the Princess to be stolen, and as the King had only one enemy of whom anybody knew, and he was the King across the river, she thought the Princess must be there.

" It seems very likely," said the Baron after she had finished, " but if she is there it is hopeless. Our King could never conquer the other one, who has a much stronger army."

" Do you know," asked the Pop-corn man, " if they have ever had any pop-corn on the other side of the river ? "

" I don't think they have," replied the Baron.

" Then," said the Pop-corn man, " I think I can free the Princess."

" You ! " cried the Baron scornfully.

But the Pop-corn man said nothing more. He bowed low to the Baron and the Head-nurse, and left the tower.

" The idea of his talking as he did," said the Baron. But the nurse was pinning her shawl, and she hurried out of the tower and overtook the Pop-corn man.

" How are you going to manage it ? " whispered she, touching his sleeve.

The Pop-corn man started. " Oh, it's you ? " he said. " Well, you wait a little, and you will see. Do you suppose you could find six little boys who would be willing to go over the river with me to-morrow?"

"Would it be quite safe?"

"Quite safe."

"I have six little brothers who would go," said the Head-nurse.

So it was arranged that the six little brothers should go across the river with the Pop-corn man; and the next morning they set out. They were all decorated with strings of Pop-corn, they carried baskets of pop-corn, and bore corn-poppers over their shoulders, and they crossed the river in a row boat.

Once over the river they went about peddling pop-corn. The man sent the boys all over the city, but he himself went straight to the palace.

He knocked at the palace-door, and the maid-servant came. "Is the King at home?" asked the Pop-corn man.

The maid said he was, and the Pop-corn man asked to see him. Just then a baby cried.

"What baby is that crying?" asked he.

"A baby that was brought here at sunset, several months ago," replied the maid; and he knew at once that he had found the Princess.

"Will you find out if I can see the King?" he said.

"I'll see," answered the maid. And she went in to find the King. Pretty soon she returned and asked

"YOU!" CRIED THE BARON SCORNFULLY.

the Pop-corn man to step into the parlor, which he did, and soon the King came downstairs.

The Pop-corn man displayed his wares, and the King tasted. He had never seen any pop-corn before, and he was both an epicure and a man of hobbies. "It is the nicest food that ever I tasted," he declared, and he bought all the man's stock.

"I can buy corn for you for seed, and I can order poppers enough to supply the city," suggested the Pop-corn man.

"So do," cried the King. And he gave orders for seven ships' cargoes of seed corn and fifty of poppers. "My people shall eat nothing else," said the King, "and the whole kingdom shall be planted with it. I am satisfied that it is the best national food."

That day the court dined on pop-corn, and as it was very light and unsatisfying, they had to eat a long time. They were all the afternoon dining. Right after dinner the King wrote out his royal decree that all the inhabitants should that year plant pop-corn instead of any other grain or any vegetable, and that as soon as the ships arrived they should make it their only article of food. For the King, when he had learned from the Pop-corn man that the corn needed to be not only ripe but well dried before it would pop, could not wait, but had ordered five hundred cargoes of pop-corn for immediate use.

So as soon as the ships arrived the people began

at once to pop corn and eat it. There was a sound of popping corn all over the city, and the people popped all day long. It was necessary that they should, because it took such a quantity to satisfy hunger, and when they were not popping they had to eat. People shook the poppers until their arms were tired, then gave them to others, and sat down to eat. Men, women and children popped. It was all that they could do, with the exception of planting the seed-corn, and then they were faint with hunger as they worked. The stores and schools were closed. In the palace the King and Queen themselves were obliged to pop in order to secure enough to eat, and the nobles and the court-ladies toiled and ate, day and night. But the little stolen Princess and the King's son, the little Prince, could not pop corn, for they were only babies.

When the people across the river had been popping corn for about a month, the Pop-corn man went to the King of Romalia's palace, and sought an audience. He told him how he had discovered his daughter in the palace of the King across the river.

The King of Romalia clasped his hands in despair. " I must make war," said he, " but my army is nothing to his."

However, he at once went about making war. He ordered the swords to be cleaned with sand-paper until they shone, and new bullets to be cast. The

Bee Guards were drilled every day, and the people could not sleep for the drums and the fifes.

When everything was ready the King of Romalia and his army crossed the river and laid siege to the city. They had expected to have the passage of the river opposed, but not a foeman was stationed on the opposite

BOTH THE KING AND QUEEN WERE OBLIGED TO POP

bank. All the spears they could see were the waving green ones of pop-corn fields. They marched straight up to the city walls and laid siege. The inhabitants fought on the walls and in the gate-towers, but not very many could fight at a time, because they would have to stop and pop corn and eat.

The defenders grew fewer and fewer, some were killed, and all of them were growing too tired and weak to fight. They could not eat enough pop-corn to give them strength and have any time left to fight. They filled their pockets and tried to eat pop-corn as they fought, but they could not manage that very well.

On the third day the city surrendered with very little loss of life on either side, and the little Princess Rosetta was restored to her parents. There was great rejoicing all through Romalia; in the evening there was an illumination and a torch-light procession. The nurses marched with their bonnets on the right way, and the Knights of the Golden Bee were out in full regalia.

The next day the Head-nurse was married, and the King gave her a farm and a dozen bee-hives for a wedding present, and the Queen a beautiful bridal bonnet trimmed with white plumes and hollyhocks.

All the court, the Baron and the Pop-corn man went to the wedding, and wedding-cake and corn-balls were passed around.

After the wedding the Pop-corn man went home. He lived in another country on the other side of a mountain. The King pressed him to take some reward. " I am puzzled," he said to the Pop-corn man, " to know what to offer you. The usual reward in such cases is the hand of the Princess in marriage, but

Rosetta is not a year old. If there is anything else you can think of." —

The Pop-corn man kissed the King's hand and replied that there was nothing that he could think of except a little honey-comb. He should like to carry some to his mother. So the King gave him a great piece of honey-comb in a silver dish, and the Pop-corn man departed.

He never came to Romalia again, but the Poet Laureate celebrated him in an epic poem, describing the loss of the Princess and the war for her rescue. The Princess was never stolen again — indeed the necromancer across the river who had kidnaped her was imprisoned for life on a diet of pop-corn which he popped himself.

The King across the river became tired of pop-corn, as it had caused his defeat, and forbade his people to eat it. He paid tribute to the King of Romalia as long as he lived; but after his death, when his son, the young prince, came to reign, affairs were on a very pleasant footing between the two kingdoms. The new King was very different from his father, being generous and amiable, and beloved by every one. Indeed Rosetta, when she had grown to be a beautiful maiden, married him and went to live as a Queen where she had been a captive.

And when Rosetta went across the river to live, the King, her father, gave her some bee-hives for a wedding present, and the bees thrived equally in both countries. All the difference in the honey was this: in Romalia the bees fed more on clover, and the honey tasted of clover: and in the country across the river on peppermint, and that honey tasted of peppermint. They always had both kinds at their Bee Festivals.

THE CHRISTMAS MONKS.

ALL children have wondered unceasingly from their very first Christmas up to their very last Christmas, where the Christmas presents come from. It is very easy to say that Santa Claus brought them. All well regulated people know that, of course; but the reindeer, and the sledge, and the pack crammed with toys, the chimney, and all the rest of it — that is all true, of course, and everybody knows about it; but that is not the question which puzzles. What children want to know is, where do these Christmas presents come from in the first place? Where does Santa Claus get them? Well the answer to that is, *In the garden of the Christmas Monks.* This has not been known until very lately; that is, it has not been known till very lately except in the immediate vicinity of the Christmas Monks. There, of course, it has been known for ages. It is rather an out-of-the-way place; and that accounts for our never hearing of it before.

The Convent of the Christmas Monks is a most charmingly picturesque pile of old buildings; there are towers and turrets, and peaked roofs and arches, and everything which could possibly be thought of in

69

the architectural line, to make a convent picturesque. It is built of graystone ; but it is only once in a while that you can see the graystone, for the walls are almost completely covered with mistletoe and ivy and ever-green. There are the most delicious little arched windows with diamond panes peeping out from the mistletoe and evergreen, and always at all times of the year, a little Christmas wreath of ivy and holly-berries is suspended in the center of every window. Over all the doors, which are likewise arched, are Christmas garlands, and over the main entrance *Merry Christmas* in evergreen letters.

The Christmas Monks are a jolly brethren ; the robes of their order are white, gilded with green gar-lands, and they never are seen out at any time of the year without Christmas wreaths on their heads. Every morning they file in a long procession into the chapel, to sing a Christmas carol; and every even-ing they ring a Christmas chime on the convent bells. They eat roast turkey and plum pudding and mince-pie for dinner all the year round ; and always carry what is left in baskets trimmed with evergreen, to the poor people. There are always wax candles lighted and set in every window of the convent at nightfall; and when the people in the country about get uncom-monly blue and down-hearted, they always go for a cure to look at the Convent of the Christmas Monks after the candles are lighted and the chimes are ring-

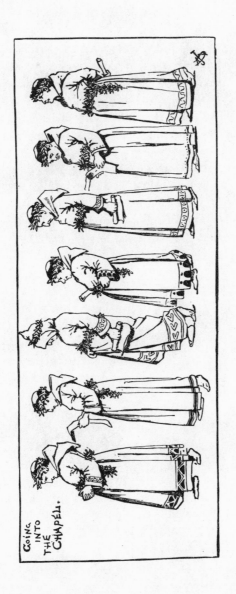

GOING INTO THE CHAPEL.

ing. It brings to mind things which never fail to cheer them.

But the principal thing about the Convent of the Christmas Monks is the garden; for that is where the Christmas presents grow. This garden extends over a large number of acres, and is divided into different departments, just as we divide our flower and vegetable gardens; one bed for onions, one for cabbages, and one for phlox, and one for verbenas, etc.

Every spring the Christmas Monks go out to sow the Christmas-present seeds after they have ploughed the ground and made it all ready.

There is one enormous bed devoted to rocking-horses. The rocking-horse seed is curious enough; just little bits of rocking-horses so small that they can only be seen through a very, very powerful microscope. The Monks drop these at quite a distance from each other, so that they will not interfere while growing; then they cover them up neatly with earth, and put up a sign-post with " Rocking-horses " on it in evergreen letters. Just so with the penny-trumpet seed, and the toy-furniture seed, the skate-seed, the sled-seed, and all the others.

Perhaps the prettiest and most interesting part of the garden, is that devoted to wax dolls. There are other beds for the commoner dolls — for the rag dolls, and the china dolls, and the rubber dolls, but of course wax dolls would look much handsomer growing. Wax dolls have to be planted quite early in the season; for they need a good start before the sun is very high. The seeds are the loveliest bits of microscopic dolls imaginable. The Monks sow them pretty close together, and they begin to come up by the middle of May. There is first just a little glimmer of gold, or flaxen, or black, or brown as the case may be, above the soil. Then the snowy foreheads appear, and the blue eyes, and black eyes, and, later on, all those enchanting little heads are out of the ground, and are nodding and winking and smiling to each other the whole extent of the field ; with their pinky cheeks and sparkling eyes and curly hair there is nothing so pretty as these little wax doll heads peeping out of the earth. Gradually, more and more of them come to light, and finally by Christmas they are all ready to gather. There they stand, swaying to and fro, and dancing lightly on their slender feet which are connected with the ground, each by a tiny green stem ; their dresses of pink, or blue, or white — for their dresses grow with them — flutter in the air. Just about the prettiest sight in the world, is the bed of wax dolls in the garden of the Christmas Monks at Christmas time.

Of course ever since this convent and garden were established (and that was so long ago that the wisest man can find no books about it) their glories have attracted a vast deal of admiration and curiosity from the young people in the surrounding country; but as the garden is enclosed on all sides by an immensely thick and high hedge, which no boy could climb, or peep over, they could only judge of the garden by the fruits which were parcelled out to them on Christmas-day.

You can judge, then, of the sensation among the young folks, and older ones, for that matter, when one evening there appeared hung upon a conspicuous place in the garden-hedge, a broad strip of white cloth trimmed with evergreen and printed with the following notice in evergreen letters:

" WANTED : — By the Christmas Monks, two *good* boys to assist in garden work. Applicants will be examined by Fathers Anselmus and Ambrose, in the convent refectory, on April 10th."

This notice was hung out about five o'clock in the evening, some time in the early part of February. By noon, the street was so full of boys staring at it with their mouths wide open, so as to see better, that the king was obliged to send his bodyguard before him to clear the way with brooms, when he wanted to pass on his way from his chamber of state to his palace.

There was not a boy in the country but looked upon this position as the height of human felicity. To work all the year in that wonderful garden, and see those wonderful things growing! and without doubt any boy who worked there could have all the toys he wanted, just as a boy who works in a candy-shop always has all the candy he wants!

But the great difficulty, of course, was about the degree of goodness requisite to pass the examination. The boys in this country were no worse than the boys in other countries, but there were not many of them that would not have done a little differently if he had only known beforehand of the advertisement of the Christmas Monks. However, they made the most of the time remaining, and were so good all over the kingdom that a very millennium seemed dawning. The school teachers used their ferrules for fire wood, and the King ordered all the birch-trees cut down and exported, as he thought there would be no more call for them in his own realm.

When the time for the examination drew near, there were two boys whom every one thought would obtain the situation, although some of the other boys had lingering hopes for themselves ; if only the Monks would examine them on the last six weeks, they thought they might pass. Still all the older people had decided in their minds that the Monks would choose these two boys. One was the Prince, the King's oldest son ; and the other was a poor boy named Peter. The Prince was no better than the other boys ; indeed, to tell the truth, he was not so good ; in fact, was the biggest rogue in the whole country ; but all the lords and the ladies, and all the

THE BOYS' READ THE NOTICE.

people who admired the lords and ladies, said it was
their solemn belief that the Prince was the best boy
in the whole kingdom ; and they were prepared to give
in their testimony, one and all, to that effect to the
Christmas Monks.

Peter was really and truly such a good boy that
there was no excuse for saying he was not. His
father and mother were poor people ; and Peter
worked every minute out of school hours, to help them
along. Then he had a sweet little crippled sister
whom he was never tired of caring for. Then, too,
he contrived to find time to do lots of little kindnesses
for other people. He always studied his lessons faithfully, and never ran away from school. Peter was
such a good boy, and so modest and unsuspicious that
he was good, that everybody loved him. He had not
the least idea that he could get the place with the
Christmas Monks, but the Prince was sure of it.

When the examination day came all the boys from
far and near, with their hair neatly brushed and
parted, and dressed in their best clothes, flocked into
the convent. Many of their relatives and friends went
with them to witness the examination.

The refectory of the convent where they assembled,
was a very large hall with a delicious smell of roast
turkey and plum pudding in it. All the little boys
sniffed, and their mouths watered.

The two fathers who were to examine the boys were

perched up in a high pulpit so profusely trimmed with
evergreen that it looked like a bird's nest ; they were
remarkably pleasant-looking men, and their eyes
twinkled merrily under their Christmas wreaths.
Father Anselmus was a little the taller of the two, and
Father Ambrose was a little the broader ; and that
was about all the difference between them in looks.

The little boys all stood up in a row, their friends
stationed themselves in good places, and the examination began.

Then if one had been placed beside the entrance to
the convent, he would have seen one after another, a
crestfallen little boy with his arm lifted up and
crooked, and his face hidden in it, come out and walk
forlornly away. He had failed to pass.

The two fathers found out that this boy had robbed
birds' nests, and this one stolen apples. And one
after another they walked disconsolately away till there
were only two boys left : the Prince and Peter.

" Now, your Highness," said Father Anselmus, who
always took the lead in the questions, " are you a good
boy ? "

" O holy Father ! " exclaimed all the people —
there were a good many fine folks from the court
present. " He is such a good boy ! such a wonderful
boy ! we never knew him to do a wrong thing."

" I don't suppose he ever robbed a bird's nest ? "
said Father Ambrose a little doubtfully.

THE PRINCE &
PETER ARE EX-
AMINED BY THE
MONKS.

" No, no ! " chorused the people.

" Nor tormented a kitten ? "

" No, no, no ! " cried they all.

At last everybody being so confident that there could be no reasonable fault found with the Prince, he was pronounced competent to enter upon the Monks' service.　Peter they knew a great deal about before — indeed a glance at his face was enough to satisfy any one of his goodness ; for he did look more like one of the boy angels in the altar-piece than anything else. So after a few questions, they accepted him also ; and the people went home and left the two boys with the Christmas Monks.

The next morning Peter was obliged to lay aside his homespun coat, and the Prince his velvet tunic, and both were dressed in some little white robes with ever-green girdles like the Monks.　Then the Prince was set to sewing Noah's Ark seed, and Peter picture-book seed.　Up and down they went scattering the seed. Peter sang a little psalm to himself, but the Prince grumbled because they had not given him gold-watch or gem seed to plant instead of the toy which he had outgrown long ago.　By noon Peter had planted all his picture-books, and fastened up the card to mark them on the pole ; but the Prince had dawdled so his work was not half done.

" We are going to have a trial with this boy," said the Monks to each other ; " we shall have to set him a penance at once, or we cannot manage him at all."

So the Prince had to go without his dinner, and kneel on dried peas in the chapel all the afternoon. The next day he finished his Noah's Arks meekly; but the next day he rebelled again and had to go the whole length of the field where they planted jewsharps, on his knees. And so it was about every other day for the whole year.

One of the brothers had to be set apart in a meditating cell to invent new penances ; for they had used up all on their list before the Prince had been with them three months.

The Prince became dreadfully tired of his convent life, and if he could have brought it about would have run away. Peter, on the contrary, had never been so happy in his life. He worked like a bee, and the pleasure he took in seeing the lovely things he had planted come up, was unbounded, and the Christmas carols and chimes delighted his soul. Then, too, he had never fared so well in his life. He could never remember the time before when he had been a whole week without being hungry. He sent his wages every month to his parents ; and he never ceased to wonder at the discontent of the Prince.

"They grow so slow," the Prince would say, wrinkling up his handsome forehead. " I expected to have a bushelful of new toys every month ; and not one have I had yet. And these stingy old Monks say I can only have my usual Christmas share anyway, nor can I pick them out myself. I never saw such a stupid place to stay in in my life. I want to have my velvet tunic on and go home to the palace and ride on my white pony with the silver tail, and hear them all tell me how charming I am." Then the Prince would crook his arm and put his head on it and cry.

Peter pitied him, and tried to comfort him, but it was not of much use, for the Prince got angry because he was not discontented as well as himself.

Two weeks before Christmas everything in the garden was nearly ready to be picked. Some few things needed a little more December sun, but everything looked perfect. Some of the Jack-in-the-boxes would not pop out quite quick enough, and some of the jumping-Jacks were hardly as limber as they might be as yet; that was all. As it was so near Christmas the Monks were engaged in their holy exercises in the chapel for the greater part of the time, and only went over the garden once a day to see if everything was all right.

The Prince and Peter were obliged to be there all the time. There was plenty of work for them to do; for once in a while something would blow over, and then there were the penny-trumpets to keep in tune; and that was a vast sight of work.

One morning the Prince was at one end of the

garden straightening up some wooden soldiers which had toppled over, and Peter was in the wax doll bed dusting the dolls. All of a sudden he heard a sweet little voice : " O, Peter ! " He thought at first one of the dolls was talking, but they could not say anything but papa and mamma; and had the merest apologies for voices anyway. " Here I am, Peter ! " and there was a little pull at his sleeve. There was his little sister. She was not any taller than the dolls around her, and looked uncommonly like the prettiest, pinkest-cheeked, yellowest-haired ones ; so it was no wonder that Peter did not see her at first. She stood there poising herself on her crutches, poor little thing, and smiling lovingly up at Peter.

" Oh, you darling ! " cried Peter, catching her up in his arms. " How did you get in here? "

" I stole in behind one of the Monks," said she " I saw him going up the street past our house, and 1 ran out and kept behind him all the way. When he opened the gate I whisked in too, and then I followed him into the garden. I've been here with the dollies ever since."

" Well," said poor Peter, " I don't see what I am going to do with you, now you are here. I can't let you out again; and I don't know what the Monks will say."

" Oh, I know ! " cried the little girl gayly. " I'll stay out here in the garden. I can sleep in one of

THE BOYS AT
WORK IN
THE
CONVENT
GARDEN.

those beautiful dolls' cradles over there ; and you can bring me something to eat."

" But the Monks come out every morning to look over the garden, and they'll be sure to find you," said her brother, anxiously.

" No, I'll hide! O, Peter, here is a place where there isn't any doll! "·

" Yes; that doll didn't come up."

" Well, I'll tell you what I'll do ! I'll just stand here in this place where the doll didn't come up, and nobody can tell the difference."

" Well, I don't know but you can do that," said Peter, although he was still ill at ease. He was so good a boy he was very much afraid of doing wrong, and offending his kind friends the Monks ; at the same time he could not help being glad to see his dear little sister.

He smuggled some food out to her, and she played merrily about him all day ; and at night he tucked her into one of the dolls' cradles with lace pillows and quilt of rose-colored silk.

The next morning when the Monks were going the rounds, the father who inspected the wax doll bed, was a bit nearsighted, and he never noticed the difference between the dolls and Peter's little sister, who swung herself on her crutches, and looked just as much like a wax doll as she possibly could. So the two were delighted with the success of their plan.

They went on thus for a few days, and Peter could not help being happy with his darling little sister, although at the same time he could not help worrying for fear he was doing wrong.

Something else happened now, which made him worry still more; the Prince ran away. He had been watching for a long time for an opportunity to possess himself of a certain long ladder made of twisted evergreen ropes, which the Monks kept locked up in the toolhouse. Lately, by some oversight, the toolhouse had been left unlocked one day, and the Prince got the ladder. It was the latter part of the afternoon, and the Christmas Monks were all in the chapel practicing Christmas carols. The Prince found a very large hamper, and picked as many Christmas presents for himself as he could stuff into it; then he put the ladder against the high gate in front of the convent, and climbed up, dragging the hamper after him. When he reached the top of the gate, which was quite broad, he sat down to rest for a moment before pulling the ladder up so as to drop it on the other side.

He gave his feet a little triumphant kick as he looked back at his prison, and down slid the evergreen ladder! The Prince lost his balance, and would inevitably have broken his neck if he had not clung desperately to the hamper which hung over on the convent side of the fence ; and as it was just the same weight as the Prince, it kept him suspended on the other.

He screamed with all the force of his royal lungs; was heard by a party of noblemen who were gallop- ing up the street; was rescued, and carried in state to the palace. But he was obliged to drop the hamper of presents, for with it all the ingenuity of the noble- men could not rescue him as speedily as it was neces- sary they should.

When the good Monks discovered the escape of the Prince they were greatly grieved, for they had tried their best to do well by him; and poor Peter could with difficulty be comforted. He had been very fond of the Prince, although the latter had done little ex- cept torment him for the whole year; but Peter had a way of being fond of folks.

A few days after the Prince ran away, and the day before the one on which the Christmas presents were to be gathered, the nearsighted father went out into the wax doll field again; but this time he had his spectacles on, and could see just as well as any one, and even a little better. Peter's little sister was swinging herself on her crutches, in the place where the wax doll did not come up, tipping her little face up, and smiling just like the dolls around her.

"Why, what is this!" said the father. "*Hoc credam!* I thought that wax doll did not come up. Can my eyes deceive me? *non verum est!* There is a doll there — and what a doll! on crutches, and in poor, homely gear!"

Then the nearsighted father put out his hand toward Peter's little sister. She jumped — she could not help it, and the holy father jumped too; the Christmas wreath actually tumbled off his head.

"It is a miracle!" exclaimed he when he could speak; "the little girl is alive! *parra puella viva est.* I will pick her and take her to the brethren, and we will pay her the honors she is entitled to."

Then the good father put on his Christmas wreath, for he dared not venture before his abbot without it, picked up Peter's little sister, who was trembling in all her little bones, and carried her into the chapel, where the Monks were just assembling to sing another carol. He went right up to the Christmas abbot, who was seated in a splendid chair, and looked like a king.

"Most holy abbot," said the nearsighted father, holding out Peter's little sister, "behold a miracle, *vide miraculum!* Thou wilt remember that there was one wax doll planted which did not come up. Behold, in her place I have found this doll on crutches, which is — alive!"

"Let me see her!" said the abbot; and all the other Monks crowded around, opening their mouths just like the little boys around the notice, in order to see better.

"*Verum est,*" said the abbot. "It is verily a miracle."

"Rather a lame miracle," said the brother who

had charge of the funny picture-books and the toy monkeys; they rather threw his mind off its level of sobriety, and he was apt to make frivolous speeches unbecoming a monk.

THE PRINCE RUNS AWAY

The abbot gave him a reproving glance, and the brother, who was the leach of the convent, came forward. "Let me look at the miracle, most holy abbot," said he. He took up Peter's sister, and looked carefully at the small, twisted ankle. "I think I can cure this with my herbs and simples," said he.

"But I don't know," said the abbot doubtfully. "I never heard of curing a miracle."

"If it is not lawful, my humble power will not suffice to cure it," said the father who was the leach.

"True," said the abbot; "take her, then, and exercise thy healing art upon her, and we will go on with our Christmas devotions, for which we should now feel all the more zeal." So the father took away Peter's little sister, who was still too frightened to speak.

The Christmas Monk was a wonderful doctor, for by Christmas Eve the little girl was completely cured of her lameness. This may seem incredible, but it was owing in great part to the herbs and simples, which are of a species that our doctors have no knowledge of; and also to a wonderful lotion which has never been advertised on our fences.

Peter of course heard the talk about the miracle, and knew at once what it meant. He was almost heartbroken to think he was deceiving the Monks so, but at the same time he did not dare to confess the truth for fear they would put a penance upon his sister, and he could not bear to think of her having to kneel upon dried peas.

He worked hard picking Christmas presents, and hid his unhappiness as best he could. On Christmas

Eve he was called into the chapel. The Christmas Monks were all assembled there. The walls were covered with green garlands and boughs and sprays of hollyberries, and branches of wax lights were gleaming brightly amongst them. The altar and the picture of the Blessed Child behind it were so bright as to almost dazzle one; and right up in the midst of it, in a lovely white dress, all wreaths and jewels, in a little chair with a canopy woven of green branches over it, sat Peter's little sister.

And there were all the Christmas Monks in their white robes and wreaths, going up in a long procession, with their hands full of the very showiest Christmas presents to offer them to her!

But when they reached her and held out the lovely presents — the first was an enchanting wax doll, the biggest beauty in the whole garden — instead of reaching out her hands for them, she just drew back, and said in her little sweet, piping voice : " Please, I ain't a millacle, I'm only Peter's little sister."

" Peter ? " said the abbot ; " the Peter who works in our garden ? "

" Yes," said the little sister.

Now here was a fine opportunity for a whole convent full of monks to look foolish — filing up in procession with their hands full of gifts to offer to a miracle, and finding there was no miracle, but only Peter's little sister.

But the abbot of the Christmas Monks had always maintained that there were two ways of looking at all things ; if any object was not what you wanted it to be in one light, that there was another light in which it would be sure to meet your views.

So now he brought this philosophy to bear.

" This little girl did not come up in the place of the wax doll, and she is not a miracle in that light," said he ; " but look at her in another light and she is a miracle — do you not see ? "

They all looked at her, the darling little girl, the very meaning and sweetness of all Christmas in her loving, trusting, innocent face.

" Yes," said all the Christmas Monks, " she is a miracle." And they all laid their beautiful Christmas presents down before her.

Peter was so delighted he hardly knew himself ; and, oh ! the joy there was when he led his little sister home on Christmas-day, and showed all the wonderful presents.

The Christmas Monks always retained Peter in their employ — in fact he is in their employ to this day. And his parents, and his little sister who was entirely cured of her lameness, have never wanted for anything.

As for the Prince, the courtiers were never tired of discussing and admiring his wonderful knowledge of physics which led to his adjusting the weight of the

hamper of Christmas presents to his own so nicely
that he could not fall. The Prince liked the talk and
the admiration well enough, but he could not help,
also, being a little glum; for he got no Christmas
presents that year.

THE PUMPKIN GIANT.

A very long time ago, before our grandmother's time, or our great-grandmother's, or our grandmothers' with a very long string of greats prefixed, there were no pumpkins; people had never eaten a pumpkin-pie, or even stewed pumpkin ; and that was the time when the Pumpkin Giant flourished.

There have been a great many giants who have flourished since the world begun, and although a select few of them have been good giants, the majority of them have been so bad that their crimes even more than their size have gone to make them notorious. But the Pumpkin Giant was an uncommonly bad one, and his general appearance and his behavior were such as to make one shudder to an extent that you would hardly believe possible. The convulsive shivering caused by the mere mention of his name, and, in some cases where the people were unusually sensitive, by the mere thought of him even, more resembled the blue ague than anything else ; indeed was known by the name of " the Giant's Shakes."

The Pumpkin Giant was very tall; he probably would have overtopped most of the giants you have

ever heard of. I don't suppose the Giant who lived
on the Bean-stalk whom Jack visited, was anything
to compare with him ; nor that it would have been a
possible thing for the Pumpkin Giant, had he received
an invitation to spend an afternoon with the Bean-
stalk Giant, to accept, on account of his inability to
enter the Bean-stalk Giant's door, no matter how
much he stooped.

The Pumpkin Giant had a very large yellow head,
which was also smooth and shiny. His eyes were big
and round, and glowed like coals of fire ; and you
would almost have thought that his head was lit up
inside with candles. Indeed there was a rumor to
that effect amongst the common people, but that was
all nonsense, of course ; no one of the more enlight-
ened class credited it for an instant. His mouth,
which stretched half around his head, was furnished
with rows of pointed teeth, and he was never known to
hold it any other way than wide open.

The Pumpkin Giant lived in a castle, as a matter
of course ; it is not fashionable for a giant to live in
any other kind of a dwelling — why, nothing would
be more tame and uninteresting than a giant in a two-
story white house with green blinds and a picket fence,
or even a brown-stone front, if he could get into either
of them, which he could not.

The Giant's castle was situated on a mountain, as
it ought to have been, and there was also the usual

courtyard before it, and the customary moat, which was full of — *bones !* All I have got to say about these bones is, they were not mutton bones. A great many details of this story must be left to the imagination of the reader ; they are too harrowing to relate. A much tenderer regard for the feelings of the audience will be shown in this than in most giant stories ; we will even go so far as to state in advance, that the story has a good end, thereby enabling readers to peruse it comfortably without unpleasant suspense.

The Pumpkin Giant was fonder of little boys and girls than anything else in the world ; but he was somewhat fonder of little boys, and more particularly of *fat* little boys.

The fear and horror of this Giant extended over the whole country. Even the King on his throne was so severely afflicted with the Giant's Shakes that he had been obliged to have the throne propped, for fear it should topple over in some unusually violent fit. There was good reason why the King shook: his only daughter, the Princess Ariadne Diana, was probably the fattest princess in the whole world at that date. So fat was she that she had never walked a step in the dozen years of her life, being totally unable to progress over the earth by any method except rolling. And a really beautiful sight it was, too, to see the Princess Ariadne Diana, in her cloth-of-gold rolling-suit, faced with green velvet and edged with ermine,

with her glittering crown on her head, trundling along
the avenues of the royal gardens, which had been furnished with strips of rich carpeting for her express
accommodation.

But gratifying as it would have been to the King,
her sire, under other circumstances, to have had such
an unusually interesting daughter, it now only served
to fill his heart with the greatest anxiety on her account. The Princess was never allowed to leave the
palace without a body-guard of fifty knights, the very
flower of the King's troops, with lances in rest, but in
spite of all this precaution, the King shook.

Meanwhile amongst the ordinary people who could
not procure an escort of fifty armed knights for the
plump among their children, the ravages of the Pumpkin Giant were frightful. It was apprehended at one
time that there would be very few fat little girls, and
no fat little boys at all, left in the kingdom. And
what made matters worse, at that time the Giant commenced taking a tonic to increase his appetite.

Finally the King, in desperation, issued a proclamation that he would knight any one, be he noble or
common, who should cut off the head of the Pumpkin
Giant. This was the King's usual method of reward-
ing any noble deed in his kingdom. It was a cheap
method, and besides everybody liked to be a knight.

When the King issued his proclamation every man
in the kingdom who was not already a knight, straight-

way tried to contrive ways and means to kill the
Pumpkin Giant. But there was one obstacle which
seemed insurmountable : they were afraid, and all of
them had the Giant's Shakes so badly, that they could
not possibly have held a knife steady enough to cut
off the Giant's head, even if they had dared to go near
enough for that purpose.

There was one man who lived not far from the
terrible Giant's castle, a poor man, his only worldly
wealth consisting in a large potato-field and a cottage
in front of it. But he had a boy of twelve, an only
son, who rivaled the Princess Ariadne Diana in point
of fatness. He was unable to have a body-guard for
his son ; so the amount of terror which the inhabitants
of that humble cottage suffered day and night was
heart-rending. The poor mother had been unable to
leave her bed for two years, on account of the Giant's
Shakes; her husband barely got a living from the
potato-field; half the time he and his wife had hardly
enough to eat, as it naturally took the larger part of
the potatoes to satisfy the fat little boy, their son, and
their situation was truly pitiable.

The fat boy's name was Æneas, his father's name
was Patroclus, and his mother's Daphne. It was all
the fashion in those days to have classical names.
And as that was a fashion as easily adopted by the
poor as the rich, everybody had them. They were
just like Jim and Tommy and May in these days.

Why, the Princess's name, Ariadne Diana, was nothing more nor less than Ann Eliza with us.

One morning Patroclus and Æneas were out in the field digging potatoes, for new potatoes were just in the market. The Early Rose potato had not been discovered in those days; but there was another potato, perhaps equally good, which attained to a similar degree of celebrity. It was called the Young Plantagenet, and reached a very large size indeed, much larger than the Early Rose does in our time.

Well, Patroclus and Æneas had just dug perhaps a bushel of Young Plantagenet potatoes. It was slow work with them, for Patroclus had the Giant's Shakes badly that morning, and of course Æneas was not very swift. He rolled about among the potato-hills after the manner of the Princess Ariadne Diana; but he did not present as imposing an appearance as she, in his homespun farmer's frock.

All at once the earth trembled violently. Patroclus and Æneas looked up and saw the Pumpkin Giant coming with his mouth wide open. "Get behind me, O, my darling son!" cried Patroclus.

Æneas obeyed, but it was of no use; for you could see his cheeks each side his father's waistcoat.

Patroclus was not ordinarily a brave man, but he was brave in an emergency; and as that is the only time when there is the slightest need of bravery, it was just as well.

The Pumpkin Giant strode along faster and faster, opening his mouth wider and wider, until they could fairly hear it crack at the corners.

Then Patroclus picked up an enormous Young Plantagenet and threw it plump into the Pumpkin Giant's mouth. The Giant choked and gasped, and choked and gasped, and finally tumbled down and died.

HE PICKED UP AN ENORMOUS YOUNG PLANTAGENET AND THREW
IT AT HIM.

Patroclus and Æneas while the Giant was choking, had run to the house and locked themselves in; then they looked out of the kitchen window; when they saw the Giant tumble down and lie quite still, they knew he must be dead. Then Daphne was immediately cured of the Giant's Shakes, and got out of bed for the first time in two years. Patroclus sharpened the carving-knife on the kitchen stove, and they all went out into the potato-field.

They cautiously approached the prostrate Giant, for fear he might be shamming, and might suddenly spring up at them and — Æneas. But no, he did not move at all; he was quite dead. And, all taking turns, they hacked off his head with the carving-knife. Then Æneas had it to play with, which was quite appropriate, and a good instance of the sarcasm of destiny.

The King was notified of the death of the Pumpkin Giant, and was greatly rejoiced thereby. His Giant's Shakes ceased, the props were removed from the throne, and the Princess Ariadne Diana was allowed to go out without her body-guard of fifty knights, much to her delight, for she found them a great hindrance to the enjoyment of her daily outings.

It was a great cross, not to say an embarrassment, when she was gleefully rolling in pursuit of a charming red and gold butterfly, to find herself suddenly stopped short by an armed knight with his lance in rest.

But the King, though his gratitude for the noble deed knew no bounds, omitted to give the promised reward and knight Patroclus.

I hardly know how it happened — I don't think it was anything intentional. Patroclus felt rather hurt about it, and Daphne would have liked to be a lady,

but Æneas did not care in the least.   He had the
Giant's head to play with and that was reward enough
for him.   There was not a boy in the   neighborhood
but envied him his possession of such a unique play-
thing; and when they would stand looking over the
wall of the potato-field with longing eyes, and he was
flying over the ground with the head,
his happiness knew no bounds; and
Æneas played so much with the Giant's
head that finally late in the

THEY WERE ALL
OVER THE FIELD.

fall it got broken and scattered all over the field.
    Next spring all over Patroclus's potato-field grew
running vines, and in the fall Giant's heads.   There
they were all over the field, hundreds of them !   Then
there was consternation indeed !   The natural conclusion to be arrived at when the people saw the

yellow Giant's heads making their appearance above the ground was, that the rest of the Giants were coming.

"There was one Pumpkin Giant before," said they, "now there will be a whole army of them. If it was dreadful then what will it be in the future? If one Pumpkin Giant gave us the Shakes so badly, what will a whole army of them do?"

But when some time had elapsed and nothing more of the Giants appeared above the surface of the potato-field, and as moreover the heads had not yet displayed any sign of opening their mouths, the people began to feel a little easier, and the general excitement subsided somewhat, although the King had ordered out Ariadne Diana's body-guard again.

Now Æneas had been born with a propensity for putting everything into his mouth and tasting it; there was scarcely anything in his vicinity which could by any possibility be tasted, which he had not eaten a bit of. This propensity was so alarming in his babyhood, that Daphne purchased a book of antidotes; and if it had not been for her admirable good judgment in doing so, this story would probably never have been told; for no human baby could possibly have survived the heterogeneous diet which Æneas had indulged in. There was scarcely one of the antidotes which had not been resorted to from time to time.

Æneas had become acquainted with the peculiar flavor of almost everything in his immediate vicinity except the Giant's heads; and he naturally enough cast longing eyes at them. Night and day he wondered what a Giant's head could taste like, till finally one day when Patroclus was away he stole out into the potato-field, cut a bit out of one of the Giant's heads and ate it. He was almost afraid to, but he reflected that his mother could give him an antidote; so he ventured. It tasted very sweet and nice; he liked it so much that he cut off another piece and ate that, then another and another, until he had eaten two thirds of a Giant's head. Then he thought it was about time for him to go in and tell his mother and take an antidote, though he did not feel ill at all yet.

"Mother," said he, rolling slowly into the cottage, "I have eaten two thirds of a Giant's head, and I guess you had better give me an antidote."

"O, my precious son!" cried Daphne, "how could you?" She looked in her book of antidotes, but could not find one antidote for a Giant's head.

"O Æneas, my dear, dear son!" groaned Daphne, "there is no antidote for Giant's head! What shall we do?"

Then she sat down and wept, and Æneas wept too as loud as he possibly could. And he apparently had excellent reason to; for it did not seem possible that a boy could eat two thirds of a Giant's head and survive it without an antidote. Patroclus came home, and they told him, and he sat down and lamented with them. All day they sat weeping and watching Æneas, expecting every moment to see him die. But he did not die; on the contrary he had never felt so well in his life.

Finally at sunset Æneas looked up and laughed. "I am not going to die," said he; "I never felt so well; you had better stop crying. And I am going out to get some more of that Giant's head; I am hungry."

"Don't, don't!" cried his father and mother; but he went; for he generally took his own way, very like most only sons. He came back with a whole Giant's head in his arms.

"See here, father and mother," cried he; "we'll all have some of this; it evidently is not poison, and it is good — a great deal better than potatoes!"

Patroclus and Daphne hesitated, but they were hungry too. Since the crop of Giant's heads had sprung up in their field instead of potatoes, they had been hungry most of the time; so they tasted.

"It is good," said Daphne; "but I think it would be better cooked." So she put some in a kettle of water over the fire, and let it boil awhile; then she dished it up, and they all ate it. It was delicious. It tasted more like stewed pumpkin than anything else; in fact it was stewed pumpkin.

Daphne was inventive, and something of a genius; and next day she concocted another dish out of the Giant's heads. She boiled them, and sifted them, and mixed them with eggs and sugar and milk and spice ; then she lined some plates with puff paste, filled them with the mixture, and set them in the oven to bake.

The result was unparalleled; nothing half so exquisite had ever been tasted. They were all in ecstasies, Æneas in particular. They gathered all the Giant's heads and stored them in the cellar. Daphne baked pies of them every day, and nothing could surpass the felicity of the whole family.

One morning the King had been out hunting, and happened to ride by the cottage of Patroclus with a train of his knights. Daphne was baking pies as usual, and the kitchen door and window were both open, for the room was so warm ; so the delicious odor of the pies perfumed the whole air about the cottage.

" What is it smells so utterly lovely ? " exclaimed the King, sniffing in a rapture.

He sent his page in to see.

" The housewife is baking Giant's head pies," said the page returning.

" What ? " thundered the King. " Bring out one to me ! "

So the page brought out a pie to him, and after all

THEN THE KING KNIGHTED HIM ON THE SPOT.

his knights had tasted to be sure it was not poison, and the king had watched them sharply for a few moments to be sure they were not killed, he tasted too.

Then he beamed. It was a new sensation, and a new sensation is a great boon to a king.

" I never tasted anything so altogether superfine, so utterly magnificent in my life," cried the king ; " stewed peacocks' tongues from the Baltic, are not to be compared with it ! Call out the housewife immediately ! "

So Daphne came out trembling, and Patroclus and Æneas also.

" What a charming lad ! " exclaimed the King as his glance fell upon Æneas. " Now tell me about these wonderful pies, and I will reward you as becomes a monarch ! "

Then Patroclus fell on his knees and related the whole history of the Giant's head pies from the beginning.

The King actually blushed. " And I forgot to knight you, oh noble and brave man, and to make a lady of your admirable wife ! "

Then the King leaned gracefully down from his saddle, and struck Patroclus with his jeweled sword and knighted him on the spot.

The whole family went to live at the royal palace. The roses in the royal gardens were uprooted, and

Giant's heads . (or pumpkins, as they came to be called) were sown in their stead ; all the royal parks also were turned into pumpkin-fields.

Patroclus was in constant attendance on the King, and used to stand all day in his ante-chamber. Daphne had a position of great responsibility, for she superin- tended the baking of the pumpkin pies, and Æneas finally married the Princess Ariadne Diana.

They were wedded in great state by fifty arch- bishops ; and all the newspapers united in stating that they were the most charming and well matched young couple that had ever been united in the kingdom.

The stone entrance of the Pumpkin Giant's Castle was securely fastened, and upon it was engraved an inscription composed by the first poet in the kingdom, for which the King made him laureate, and gave him the liberal pension of fifty pumpkin pies per year.

The following is the inscription in full :

> " Here dwelt the Pumpkin Giant once,
> He's dead the nation doth rejoice,
> For, while he was alive, he lived
> By e——g dear, fat, little boys."

The inscription is said to remain to this day ; if you were to go there you would probably see it.

THE CHRISTMAS MASQUERADE.

ON Christmas Eve the Mayor's stately mansion presented a beautiful appearance. There were rows of different-colored wax candles burning in every window, and beyond them one could see the chandeliers of gold and crystal blazing with light. The fiddles were squeaking merrily, and lovely little forms flew past the windows in time to the music.

There were gorgeous carpets laid from the door to the street, and carriages were constantly arriving, and fresh guests tripping over them. They were all children. The Mayor was giving a Christmas Masquerade to-night, to all the children in the city, the poor as well as the rich. The preparation for this ball had been making an immense sensation for the last three months. Placards had been up in the most conspicuous points in the city, and all the daily newspapers had at least a column devoted to it, headed with THE MAYOR'S CHRISTMAS MASQUERADE in very large letters.

The Mayor had promised to defray the expenses of all the poor children whose parents were unable to do so, and the bills for their costumes were directed to be sent in to him.

Of course there was a great deal of excitement among the regular costumers of the city, and they all resolved to vie with one another in being the most popular, and the best patronized on this gala occasion. But the placards and the notices had not been out a week before a new Costumer appeared, who cast all the others into the shade directly. He set up his shop on the corner of one of the principal streets, and hung up his beautiful costumes in the windows. He was a little fellow, not much larger than a boy of ten. His cheeks were as red as roses, and he had on a long curling wig as white as snow. He wore a suit of crimson velvet knee-breeches, and a little swallow-tailed coat with beautiful golden buttons. Deep lace ruffles fell over his slender white hands, and he wore elegant knee-buckles of glittering stones. He sat on a high stool behind his counter and served his customers himself; he kept no clerk.

It did not take the children long to discover what beautiful things he had, and how superior he was to the other costumers, and they begun to flock to his shop immediately, from the Mayor's daughter to the poor rag-picker's. The children were to select their own costumes; the Mayor had stipulated that. It was to be a children's ball in every sense of the word.

So they decided to be fairies, and shepherdesses, and princesses, according to their own fancies; and this new costumer had charming costumes to suit them.

It was noticeable, that, for the most part, the children of the rich, who had always had everything they desired, would choose the parts of goose-girls and peasants and such like ; and the poor children jumped eagerly at the chance of being princesses or fairies for a few hours in their miserable lives.

When Christmas Eve came, and the children flocked into the Mayor's mansion, whether it was owing to the Costumer's art, or their own adaptation to the characters they had chosen, it was wonderful how lifelike their representations were. Those little fairies in their short skirts of silken gauze, in which golden sparkles appeared as they moved, with their little funny gossamer wings, like butterflies, looked like real fairies. It did not seem possible, when they floated around to the music, half supported on the tips of their dainty toes, half by their filmy, purple wings, their delicate bodies swaying in time, that they could be anything but fairies. It seemed absurd to imagine that they were Johnny Mullens, the washwoman's son, and Polly Flinders, the charwoman's little girl, and so on.

The Mayor's daughter, who had chosen the character of a goose-girl, looked so like a true one that one could hardly dream she ever was anything else. She was, ordinarily, a slender, dainty little lady, rather tall for her age. She now looked very short and stubbed and brown, just as if she had been accustomed to tend geese in all sorts of weather. It was so with all the others — the Red Riding-hoods, the princesses, the Bo Peeps, and with every one of the characters who came to the Mayor's ball ; Red Riding-hood looked round, with big, frightened eyes, all ready to spy the wolf, and carried her little pat of butter and pot of honey gingerly in her basket ; Bo Peep's eyes looked red with weeping for the loss of her sheep ; and the princesses swept about so grandly in their splendid brocaded trains, and held their crowned heads so high that people half believed them to be true princesses.

But there never was anything like the fun at the Mayor's Christmas ball. The fiddlers fiddled and fiddled, and the children danced and danced on the beautiful waxed floors. The Mayor, with his family and a few grand guests, sat on a dais covered with blue velvet at one end of the dancing hall, and watched the sport. They were all delighted. The Mayor's eldest daughter sat in front and clapped her little soft white hands. She was a tall, beautiful young maiden, and wore a white dress, and a little cap woven of blue violets on her yellow hair. Her name was Violetta.

The supper was served at midnight — and such a supper ! The mountains of pink and white ices, and the cakes with sugar castles and flower-gardens on the tops of them, and the charming shapes of gold and ruby-colored jellies ! There were wonderful bonbons

THERE NEVER WAS ANYTHING LIKE THE FUN AT THE MAYOR'S CHRISTMAS BALL.

which even the Mayor's daughter did not have every day ; and all sorts of fruits, fresh and candied. They had cowslip wine in green glasses, and elderberry wine in red, and they drank each other's health. The glasses held a thimbleful each ; the Mayor's wife thought that was all the wine they ought to have. Under each child's plate there was a pretty present ; and every one had a basket of bonbons and cake to carry home.

At four o'clock the fiddlers put up their fiddles and the children went home ; fairies and shepherdesses and pages and princesses all jabbering gleefully about the splendid time they had had.

But in a short time what consternation there was throughout the city ! When the proud and fond parents attempted to unbutton their children's dresses, in order to prepare them for bed, not a single costume would come off. The buttons buttoned again as fast as they were unbuttoned ; even if they pulled out a pin, in it would slip again in a twinkling ; and when a string was untied it tied itself up again into a bow-knot. The parents were dreadfully frightened. But the children were so tired out they finally let them go to bed in their fancy costumes, and thought perhaps they would come off better in the morning. So Red Riding-hood went to bed in her little red cloak, holding fast to her basket full of dainties for her grandmother, and Bo Peep slept with her crook in her hand.

The children all went to bed readily enough, they

were so very tired, even though they had to go in this strange array. All but the fairies — they danced and pirouetted and would not be still.

" We want to swing on the blades of grass," they

THEIR PARENTS STARED IN GREAT DISTRESS.

kept saying, " and play hide-and-seek in the lily-cups, and take a nap between the leaves of the roses."

The poor charwomen and coal-heavers, whose children the fairies were for the most part, stared at them in

great distress. They did not know what to do with
these radiant, frisky little creatures into which their
Johnnys and their Pollys and Betseys were so suddenly
transformed. But the fairies went to bed quietly
enough when daylight came, and were soon fast asleep.

There was no further trouble till twelve o'clock, when
all the children woke up. Then a great wave of alarm
spread over the city. Not one of the costumes would
come off then. The buttons buttoned as fast as they
were unbuttoned ; the pins quilted themselves in as
fast as they were pulled out ; and the strings flew
round like lightning and twisted themselves into bow-
knots as fast as they were untied.

And that was not the worst of it ; every one of the
children seemed to have become, in reality, the character
which he or she had assumed.

The Mayor's daughter declared she was going to
tend her geese out in the pasture, and the shepherdesses
sprang out of their little beds of down, throwing aside
their silken quilts, and cried that they must go out and
watch their sheep. The princesses jumped up from
their straw pallets, and wanted to go to court ; and all
the rest of them likewise. Poor little Red Riding-
hood sobbed and sobbed because she couldn't go and
carry her basket to her grandmother, and as she didn't
have any grandmother she couldn't go, of course, and
her parents were very much troubled. It was all so
mysterious and dreadful. The news spread very

rapidly over the city, and soon a great crowd gathered around the new Costumer's shop, for every one thought he must be responsible for all this mischief.

The shop door was locked; but they soon battered it down with stones. When they rushed in the Costumer was not there; he had disappeared with all his wares. Then they did not know what to do. But it was evident that they must do something before long, for the state of affairs was growing worse and worse.

The Mayor's little daughter braced her back up against the tapestried wall and planted her two feet in their thick shoes firmly. " I will go and tend my geese ! " she kept crying. " I won't eat my breakfast! I won't go out in the park ! I won't go to school. I'm going to tend my geese — I will, I will, I will ! "

And the princesses trailed their rich trains over the rough, unpainted floors in their parents' poor little huts, and held their crowned heads very high and demanded to be taken to court. The princesses were, mostly, geese-girls when they were their proper selves, and their geese were suffering, and their poor parents did not know what they were going to do, and they wrung their hands and wept as they gazed on their gorgeously-appareled children.

Finally, the Mayor called a meeting of the Aldermen, and they all assembled in the City Hall. Nearly every one of them had a son or a daughter who was a

chimney-sweep, or a little watch-girl, or a shepherdess.
They appointed a chairman and they took a great many
votes, and contrary votes ; but they did not agree on

"I WILL GO AND TEND MY GEESE!"

anything, until some one proposed that they consult
the Wise Woman.   Then they all held up their hands,
and voted to, unanimously.

So the whole board of Aldermen set out, walking by twos, with the Mayor at their head, to consult the Wise Woman. The Aldermen were all very fleshy, and carried gold-headed canes which they swung very high at every step. They held their heads well back, and their chins stiff, and whenever they met common people they sniffed gently. They were very imposing.

The Wise Woman lived in a little hut on the outskirts of the city. She kept a Black Cat; except for her, she was all alone. She was very old, and had brought up a great many children, and she was considered remarkably wise.

But when the Aldermen reached her hut and found her seated by the fire, holding her Black Cat, a new difficulty presented itself. She had always been quite deaf, and people had been obliged to scream as loud as they could in order to make her hear; but, lately, she had grown much deafer, and when the Aldermen attempted to lay the case before her she could not hear a word. In fact, she was so very deaf that she could not distinguish a tone below G-sharp. The Aldermen screamed till they were quite red in their faces, but all to no purpose; none of them could get up to G-sharp, of course.

So the Aldermen all went back, swinging their gold-headed canes, and they had another meeting in the City Hall. Then they decided to send the highest Soprano Singer in the church choir to the Wise

Woman; she could sing up to G-sharp just as easy as not. So the high-Soprano Singer set out for the Wise Woman's in the Mayor's coach, and the Aldermen marched behind, swinging their gold-headed canes.

The high-Soprano Singer put her head down close to the Wise Woman's ear, and sang all about the Christmas Masquerade, and the dreadful dilemma everybody was in, in G-sharp — she even went higher, sometimes — and the Wise Woman heard every word. She nodded three times, and every time she nodded she looked wiser.

" Go home, and give 'em a spoonful of castor-oil, all 'round," she piped up; then she took a pinch of snuff, and wouldn't say any more.

So the Aldermen went home, and each one took a district and marched through it, with a servant carrying an immense bowl and spoon, and every child had to take a dose of castor-oil.

But it didn't do a bit of good. The children cried and struggled when they were forced to take the castor-oil; but, two minutes afterward, the chimney-sweeps were crying for their brooms, and the princesses screaming because they couldn't go to court, and the Mayor's daughter, who had been given a double dose, cried louder and more sturdily: " I want to go and tend my geese! I will go and tend my geese!"

So the Aldermen took the high-Soprano Singer, and they consulted the Wise Woman again. She was taking a nap this time, and the Singer had to sing up to B-flat before she could wake her. Then she was very cross, and the Black Cat put up his back and spit at the Aldermen.

" Give 'em a spanking all 'round," she snapped out, " and if that don't work put 'em to bed without their supper ! "

Then the Aldermen marched back to try that ; and all the children in the city were spanked, and when that didn't do any good they were put to bed without any supper. But the next morning when they woke up they were worse than ever.

The Mayor and the Aldermen were very indignant, and considered that they had been imposed upon and insulted. So they set out for the Wise Woman's again, with the high-Soprano Singer.

She sang in G-sharp how the Aldermen and the Mayor considered her an imposter, and did not think she was wise at all, and they wished her to take her Black Cat and move beyond the limits of the city. She sang it beautifully ; it sounded like the very finest Italian opera-music.

" Deary me," piped the Wise Woman, when she had finished, " how very grand these gentlemen are." Her Black Cat put up his back and spit.

" Five times one Black Cat are five Black Cats," said the Wise Woman. And, directly, there were five Black Cats, spitting and miauling.

" Five times five Black Cats are twenty-five Black Cats." And then there were twenty-five of the angry little beasts.

" Five times twenty-five Black Cats are one hun-

SHE SANG IT BEAUTIFULLY.

dred and twenty-five Black Cats," added the Wise Woman, with a chuckle.

Then the Mayor and the Aldermen and the high-Soprano Singer fled precipitately out the door and back to the city. One hundred and twenty-five Black Cats had seemed to fill the Wise Woman's hut full, and when they all spit and miauled together it was dreadful. The visitors could not wait for her to multiply Black Cats any longer.

As winter wore on, and spring came, the condition of things grew more intolerable. Physicians had been consulted, who advised that the children should be allowed to follow their own bents, for fear of injury to their constitutions. So the rich Aldermen's daughters were actually out in the fields herding sheep, and their sons sweeping chimneys or carrying newspapers ; while the poor charwomen's and coal-heavers' children spent their time like princesses and fairies. Such a topsy-turvy state of society was shocking. Why, the Mayor's little daughter was tending geese out in the meadow like any common goose-girl! Her pretty elder sister, Violetta, felt very sad about it, and used often to cast about in her mind for some way of relief.

When cherries were ripe in spring, Violetta thought she would ask the Cherry-man about it. She thought the Cherry-man quite wise. He was a very pretty young fellow, and he brought cherries to sell in graceful little straw baskets lined with moss. So she stood in the kitchen-door, one morning, and told him all about the great trouble that had come upon the city. He listened in great astonishment; he had never heard of it before. He lived several miles out in the country.

"How did the Costumer look?" he asked respectfully; he thought Violetta the most beautiful lady on earth.

Then Violetta described the Costumer, and told him of the unavailing attempts that had been made to find him. There were a great many detectives out, constantly at work.

"I know where he is!" said the Cherry-man. "He's up in one of my cherry-trees. He's been living there ever since cherries were ripe, and he won't come down."

Then Violetta ran and told her father in great excitement, and he at once called a meeting of the Aldermen, and in a few hours half the city was on the road to the Cherry-man's.

He had a beautiful orchard of cherry-trees, all laden with fruit. And, sure enough, in one of the largest, way up amongst the topmost branches, sat the Costumer in his red velvet short-clothes and his diamond knee-buckles. He looked down between the green boughs. "Good-morning, friends," he shouted.

The Aldermen shook their gold-headed canes at him, and the people danced round the tree in a rage. Then they began to climb. But they soon found that to be impossible. As fast as they touched a hand or foot to the tree, back it flew with a jerk exactly as if the tree pushed it. They tried a ladder, but the ladder fell back the moment it touched the tree, and lay sprawling upon the ground. Finally, they brought axes and thought they could chop the tree down, Costumer and all ; but the wood resisted the axes as if it were iron, and only dented them, receiving no impression itself.

Meanwhile, the Costumer sat up in the tree, eating cherries, and throwing the stones down. Finally, he stood up on a stout branch and, looking down, addressed the people.

"It's of no use, your trying to accomplish anything in this way," said he ; "you'd better parley. I'm willing to come to terms with you, and make everything right, on two conditions."

The people grew quiet then, and the Mayor stepped forward as spokesman. "Name your two conditions," said he, rather testily. "You own, tacitly, that you are the cause of all this trouble."

"Well," said the Costumer, reaching out for a handful of cherries, "this Christmas Masquerade of yours was a beautiful idea; but you wouldn't do it every year, and your successors might not do it at all. I want those poor children to have a Christmas every year. My first condition is, that every poor child in the city hangs its stocking for gifts in the City Hall on every Christmas Eve, and gets it filled, too. I want the resolution filed and put away in the city archives."

"We agree to the first condition !" cried the people

with one voice, without waiting for the Mayor and Aldermen.

"The second condition," said the Costumer, "is that this good young Cherry-man here, has the Mayor's daughter, Violetta, for his wife.   He has been kind to me, letting me live in his cherry-tree, and eat his cherries, and I want to reward him."   - .

"We consent!" cried all the people ; but the Mayor, though he was so generous, was a proud man.   "I will not consent to the second condition," he cried angrily.

"Very well," replied the Costumer, picking some more cherries, "then your youngest daughter tends geese the rest of her life, that's all!"

The Mayor was in great distress ; but the thought of his youngest daughter being a goose-girl all her life was too much for him.   He gave in at last.

"Now go home, and take the costumes off your children," said the Costumer, "and leave me in peace to eat cherries!"

Then the people hastened back to the city and found, to their great delight, that the costumes would come off.   The pins staid out, the buttons staid unbuttoned, and the strings staid untied.   The children were dressed in their own proper clothes and were their own proper selves once more.   The shepherdesses and the chimney-sweeps came home, and were washed and dressed in silks and velvets, and went to embroidering and playing lawn-tennis. And the princesses and the fairies put on their own suitable dresses, and went about their useful employments. There was great rejoicing in every home. Violetta thought she had never been so happy, now that her dear little sister was no longer a goose-girl, but her own dainty little lady-self.

The resolution to provide every poor child in the city with a stocking full of gifts on Christmas was solemnly filed, and deposited in the city archives, and was never broken.

Violetta was married to the Cherry-man, and all the children came to the wedding, and strewed flowers in her path till her feet were quite hidden in them. The Costumer had mysteriously disappeared from the cherry-tree the night before, but he left, at the foot, some beautiful wedding presents for the bride — a silver service with a pattern of cherries engraved on it, and a set of china with cherries on it, in hand-painting, and a white satin robe, embroidered with cherries down the front.

DILL.

DAME CLEMENTINA was in her dairy, churning, and her little daughter Nan was out in the flower-garden. The flower-garden was a little plot back of the cottage, full of all the sweet, old-fashioned herbs. There were sweet marjoram, sage, summersavory, lavender, and ever so many others. Up in one corner, there was a little green bed of dill.

Nan was a dainty, slim little maiden, with yellow, flossy hair in short curls all over her head. Her eyes were very sweet and round and blue, and she wore a quaint little snuff-colored gown. It had a short full waist, with low neck and puffed sleeves, and the skirt was straight and narrow and down to her little heels.

She danced around the garden, picking a flower here and there. She was making a nosegay for her mother. She picked lavender and sweet-william and pinks, and bunched them up together. Finally she pulled a little sprig of dill, and ran, with that and the nosegay, to her mother in the dairy.

"Mother dear," said she, "here is a little nosegay for you; and what was it I overheard you telling Dame Elizabeth about dill last night?"

Dame Clementina stopped churning and took the nosegay. " Thank you, Sweetheart, it is lovely," said she, " and, as for the dill — it is a charmed plant, you know, like four-leaved clover."

" Do you put it over the door ? " asked Nan.

" Yes. Nobody who is envious or ill-disposed can enter into the house if there is a sprig of dill over the door. Then I know another charm which makes it stronger. If one just writes this verse :

> " ' Alva, aden, winira mir,
> Villawissen lingen;
> Sanchta, wanchta, attazir,
> Hor de mussen wingen,'

under the sprig of dill, every one envious, or evil-disposed, who attempts to enter the house, will have to stop short, just where they are, and stand there ; they cannot move."

" What does the verse mean ? " asked Nan.

" That, I do not know. It is written in a foreign language. But it is a powerful charm."

" O, mother ! will you write it off for me, if I will bring you a bit of paper and a pen ? "

" Certainly," replied her mother, and wrote it off when Nan brought pen and paper.

" Now," said she, " you must run off and play again, and not hinder me any longer, or I shall not get my butter made to-day."

So Nan danced away with the verse, and the sprig of dill, and her mother went on churning.

She had a beautiful tall stone churn, with the sides all carved with figures in relief. There were milkmaids and cows as natural as life all around the churn. The dairy was charming, too. The shelves were carved stone ; and the floor had a little silvery rill running right through the middle of it, with green ferns at the sides. All along the stone shelves were set pans full of yellow cream, and the pans were all of solid silver, with a chasing of buttercups and daisies around the brims.

It was not a common dairy, and Dame Clementina was not a common dairy-woman. She was very tall and stately, and wore her silver-white hair braided around her head like a crown, with a high silver comb at the top. She walked like a queen ; indeed she was a noble count's daughter. In her early youth, she had married a pretty young dairyman, against her father's wishes ; so she had been disinherited. The dairyman had been so very poor and low down in the world, that the count felt it his duty to cast off his daughter, lest she should do discredit to his noble line. There was a much pleasanter, easier way out of the difficulty, which the count did not see. Indeed, it was a peculiarity of all his family, that they never could see a way out of a difficulty, high and noble as they were. The count only needed to have given the poor young dairyman a few acres of his own land, and a few bags of his own gold, and begged the king, with whom he had great influence, to knight him, and all the obstacles would have been removed; the dairyman would have been quite rich and noble enough for his son-in-law. But he never thought of that, and his daughter was disinherited. However, he made all the amends to her that he could, and fitted her out royally for her humble station in life. He caused this beautiful dairy to be built for her, and gave her the silver milk-pans, and the carved stone churn.

" My daughter shall not churn in a common wooden churn, or skim the cream from wooden pans," he had said.

The dairyman had been dead a good many years now, and Dame Clementina managed the dairy alone. She never saw anything of her father, although he lived in his castle not far off, on a neighboring height. When the sky was clear, she could see its stone towers against it. She had four beautiful white cows, and Nan drove them to pasture ; they were very gentle.

When Dame Clementina had finished churning, she went into the cottage. As she stepped through the little door with clumps of sweet peas on each side, she looked up. There was the sprig of dill, and the magic verse she had written under it.

Nan was sitting at the window inside. knitting her

stent on a blue stocking. "Ah, Sweetheart," said her
mother, laughing, "you have little cause to pin the dill
and the verse over our door. None is likely to envy
us, or to be ill-disposed toward us."

"O, mother!" said Nan, "I know it, but I thought
it would be so nice to feel sure. Oh, there is Dame
Golding coming after some milk. Do you suppose she
will have to stop?"

"What nonsense!" said her mother. They both
of them watched Dame Golding coming. All of a
sudden, she stopped short, just outside. She could
go no further. She tried to lift her feet, but could
not.

"O, mother!" cried Nan, "she has stopped!"

The poor woman began to scream. She was frightened almost to death. Nan and her mother were not
much less frightened, but they did not know what to
do. They ran out, and tried to comfort her, and gave
her some cream to drink; but it did not amount to
much. Dame Golding had secretly envied Dame
Clementina for her silver milk-pans. Nan and her
mother knew why their visitor was so suddenly rooted
to the spot, of course, but she did not. She thought
her feet were paralyzed, and she kept begging them to
send for her husband.

"Perhaps he can pull her away," said Nan, crying.
How she wished she had never pinned the dill and
the verse over the door! So she set off for Dame

Golding's husband.   He came running in a great
hurry ; but when he had nearly reached his wife, and
had his arms reached out to grasp her, he, too, stopped
short.   He had envied Dame Clementina for her
beautiful white cows, and there he was fast, also.

He began to groan and scream too.   Nan and her
mother ran into the house and shut the door.   They
could not bear it.   " What shall we do, if any one else
comes ? " sobbed Nan.   " O, mother ! there is Dame
Dorothy coming.   And — yes — Oh ! she has stopped
too."   Poor Dame Dorothy had envied Dame Clementina a little for her flower-garden, which was finer
than hers, so she had to join Dame Golding and her
husband.

Pretty soon another woman came, who had looked
with envious eyes at Dame Clementina, because she
was a count's daughter ; and another, who had grudged
her a fine damask petticoat, which she had had before
she was disinherited, and still wore on holidays ; and
they both had to stop.

Then came three rough-looking men in velvet jack-
ets and slouched hats, who brought up short at the
gate with a great jerk that nearly took their breath away.
They were robbers who were prowling about with a
view to stealing Dame Clementina's silver milk-pans
some dark night.

All through the day the people kept coming and
stopping.   It was wonderful how many things poor

A STRANGE SAD STATE OF THINGS.

Dame Clementina had to be envied by men and women, and even children. They envied Nan for her yellow curls or her blue eyes, or her pretty snuff-colored gown. When the sun set, the yard in front of Dame Clementina's cottage was full of people. Lastly, just before dark, the count himself came ambling up on a coal-black horse. The count was a majestic old man dressed in velvet, with stars on his breast. His white hair fell in long curls on his shoulders, and he had a pointed beard. As he came to the gate, he caught a glimpse of Nan in the door.

" How I wish that little maiden was my child," said he. And, straightway, he stopped. His horse pawed and trembled when he lashed him with a jeweled whip to make him go on ; but he could not stir forward one step. Neither could the count dismount from his saddle ; he sat there fuming with rage.

Meanwhile, poor Dame Clementina and little Nan were overcome with distress. The sight of their yard full of all these weeping people was dreadful. Neither of them had any idea how to do away with the trouble, because of their family inability to see their way out of a difficulty.

When supper time came, Nan went for the cows, and her mother milked them into her silver milk-pails, and strained off the milk into her silver pans. Then they kindled up a fire and cooked some beautiful milk porridge for the poor people in the yard.

It was a beautiful warm moonlight night, and all the winds were sweet with roses and pinks; so the people could not suffer out of doors; but the next morning it rained.

" O, mother ! " said Nan, " it is raining, and what will the poor people do ? "

Dame Clementina would never have seen her way out of this difficulty, had not Dame Golding cried out that her bonnet was getting wet, and she wanted an umbrella.

" Why, you must go around to their houses, of course, and get their umbrellas for them," said Dame Clementina; " but first, give ours to that old man on horseback." She did not know her father, so many years had passed since she had seen him, and he had altered so.

So Nan carried out their great yellow umbrella to the count, and went around to the others' houses for their own umbrellas. It was pitiful enough to see them standing all alone behind the doors. She could not find three extra ones for the three robbers, and she felt badly about that.

Somebody suggested, however, that milk-pans turned over their heads would keep the rain off their slouched hats, at least ; so she got a silver milk-pan for an umbrella for each. They made such frantic efforts to get away then, that they looked like jumping-jacks; but it was of no use.

NAN RETURNS WITH THE UMBRELLAS.

Poor Dame Clementina and Nan after they had given the milk porridge to the people, and done all they could for their comfort, stood staring disconsolately out of the window at them under their dripping umbrellas. The yard was fairly green and black and blue and yellow with umbrellas. They wept at the sight, but they could not think of any way out of the difficulty. The people themselves might have suggested one, had they known the real cause ; but they did not dare to tell them how they were responsible for all the trouble ; they seemed so angry.

About noon Nan spied their most particular friend, Dame Elizabeth, coming. She lived a little way out of the village. Nan saw her approaching the gate through the rain and mist, with her great blue umbrella and her long blue double cape and her poke bonnet; and she cried out in the greatest dismay : " O, mother, mother ! there is our dear Dame Elizabeth coming ; she will have to stop too ! "

Then they watched her with beating hearts. ˋ Dame Elizabeth stared with astonishment at the people, and stopped to ask them questions. But she passed quite through their midst, and entered the cottage under the sprig of dill, and the verse. She did not envy Dame Clementina or Nan, anything.

" Tell me what this means," said she. " Why are all these people standing in your yard in the rain with umbrellas ? "

Then Dame Clementina and Nan told her.   " And
oh! what shall we do?" said they.   " Will these peo-

SUCH FRANTIC EFFORTS TO GET AWAY.

ple have to stand in our yard forever and ever?"
Dame Elizabeth stared at them.   The way out of

the difficulty was so plain to her, that she could not credit its not being plain to them.

" Why," said she, " don't you take down the sprig of dill and the verse ? "

" Why, sure enough ! " said they in amazement. " Why didn't we think of that before ? "

So Dame Clementina ran out quickly, and pulled down the sprig of dill and the verse.

Then the way the people hurried out of the yard ! They fairly danced and flourished their heels, old folks and all. They were so delighted to be able to move, and they wanted to be sure they could move. The robbers tried to get away unseen with their silver milk-pans, but some of the people stopped them, and set the pans safely inside the dairy. All the people, except the count, were so eager to get away, that they did not stop to inquire into the cause of the trouble then.

Afterward, when they did, they were too much ashamed to say anything about it.

It was a good lesson to them ; they were not quite so envious after that. Always, on entering any cottage, they would glance at the door, to see if, perchance, there might be a sprig of dill over it. And if there was not, they were reminded to put away any envious feeling they might have toward the inmates out of their hearts.

As for the count, he had not been so much alarmed

as the others, since he had been to the wars and was braver.   Moreover, he felt that his dignity as a noble

DAME ELIZABETH STARED WITH ASTONISHMENT.

had been insulted. So he at once dismounted and fastened his horse to the gate, and strode up to the door with his sword clanking and the plumes on his hat nodding.

"What," he begun; then he stopped short. He had recognized his daughter in Dame Clementina. She recognized him at the same moment. "O, my dear daughter!" said he. "O, my dear father!" said she.

"And this is my little grandchild?" said the count; and he took Nan upon his knee, and covered her with caresses.

Then the story of the dill and the verse was told. "Yes," said the count, "I truly was envious of you, Clementina, when I saw Nan."

After a little, he looked at his daughter sorrowfully. "I should dearly love to take you up to the castle with me, Clementina," said he, "and let you live there always, and make you and the little child my heirs. But how can I? You are disinherited, you know."

"I don't see any way," assented Dame Clementina, sadly.

Dame Elizabeth was still there, and she spoke up to the count with a curtesy.

"Noble sir," said she, "why don't you make another will?"

"Why, sure enough," cried the count with great delight, "why don't I? I'll have my lawyer up to the castle to-morrow."

He did immediately alter his will, and his daughter

was no longer disinherited.   She and Nan went to live at the castle, and were very rich and happy.   Nan learned to play on the harp, and wore snuff-colored

THE COUNT THINKS HIMSELF INSULTED.

satin gowns.   She was called Lady Nan, and she lived a long time, and everybody loved her.   But never, so long as she lived, did she pin the sprig of dill and the

verse over the door again. She kept them at the very
bottom of a little satin-wood box — the faded sprig of
dill wrapped round with the bit of paper on which was
written the charm-verse :

> " Alva, aden, winira mir,
> Villawissen lingen ;
> Sanchta, wanchta, attazir,
> Hor de mussen wingen."

THE SILVER HEN.

DAME DOROTHEA PENNY kept a private school. It was quite a small school, on account of the small size of her house. She had only twelve scholars and they filled it quite full; indeed one very little boy had to sit in the brick oven. On this account Dame Penny was obliged to do all her cooking on a Saturday when school did not keep; on that day she baked bread, and cakes, and pies enough to last a week. The oven was a very large one.

It was on a Saturday that Dame Penny first missed her silver hen. She owned a wonderful silver hen, whose feathers looked exactly as if they had been dipped in liquid silver. When she was scratching for worms out in the yard, and the sun shone on her, she was absolutely dazzling, and sent little bright reflections into the neighbors' windows, as if she were really solid silver.

Dame Penny had a sunny little coop with a padlocked door for her, and she always locked it very carefully every night. So it was doubly perplexing when the hen disappeared. Dame Penny remembered distinctly locking the coop-door; several circumstances had served to fix it on her mind. She had started out without her overshoes, then had returned for them because the snow was quite deep and she was liable to rheumatism. Then Dame Louisa who lived next door had rapped on her window, and she had run in there for a few moments with the hen-coop key dangling on its blue ribbon from her wrist, and Dame Louisa had remarked that she would lose that key if she were not more careful. Then when she returned home across the yard

THE SNOW WAS QUITE DEEP.

a doubt had seized her, and she had tried the coop-door to be sure that she had really fastened it.

The next morning when she fitted the key into the padlock and threw open the door, and no silver hen came clucking out, it was very mysterious. Dame Louisa came running to the fence which divided her yard from Dame Penny's, and stood leaning on it with her apron over her head.

"Are you sure that hen was in the coop when you locked the door?" said she.

"Of course she was in the coop," replied Dame Penny with dignity. "She has never failed to go in there at sundown for all the twenty-five years that I've had her."

Dame Penny carefully searched everywhere about the premises. When the scholars assembled she called

the school to order, and told them of her terrible loss.
All the scholars crooked their arms over their faces
and wept, for they were very fond of Dame Penny,
and also of the silver hen.   Every one of them wore
one of her silver tail-feathers in the best bonnet, or
hat, as the case might be.   The silver hen had dropped
them about the yard, and Dame Penny had presented
them from time to time as rewards for good behavior.

After Dame Penny had told the school, she tried to
proceed with the usual exercises.   But in vain.   She
whipped one little boy because he said that four and
three made seven, and she stood a little girl in the
corner because she spelled hen with one *n*.

Finally she dismissed the scholars, and gave them
permission to search for the silver hen.   She offered
the successful one the most beautiful Christmas present he had ever seen.   It was about three weeks before Christmas.

The children all put on their things, and went home
and told their parents what they were going to do ;
then they started upon the search for the silver hen.
They searched with no success till the day before
Christmas.   Then they thought they would ask Dame
Louisa, who had the reputation of being quite a wise
woman, if she knew of any more likely places in which
they could hunt.

The twelve scholars walked two by two up to Dame
Louisa's front door, and knocked.   They were very

quiet and spoke only in whispers because they knew
Dame Louisa was nervous, and did not like children
very well. Indeed it was a great cross to her that she
lived so near the school, for the scholars when out in
their own yard never thought about her nervousness,
and made a deal of noise. Then too she could hear
every time they spelled or said the multiplication-
table, or bounded the countries of Africa, and it was
very trying. To-day in spite of their efforts to be

TWO BY TWO.

quiet they awoke her from a nap, and she came to the
door, with her front-piece and cap on one side, and her
spectacles over her eyebrows, very much out of humor.

" I don't know where you'll find the hen," said she
peevishly, " unless you go to the White Woods for it."

"Thank you, ma'am," said the children with curtesies, and they all turned and went down the path between the dead Christmas-trees.

Dame Louisa had no idea that they would go to the

White Woods. She had said it quite at random, although she was so vexed in being disturbed in her nap that she wished for a moment that they would. She stood in her front door and looked at her dead Christmas-trees, and that always made her feel crosser, and she had not at any time a pleasant disposition. Indeed, it was rumored among the towns-people that that had blasted her Christmas-trees, that Dame Louisa's scolding, fretting voice had floated out to them, and smote their delicate twigs like a bitter frost and made them turn yellow; for the real Christmas-tree is not very hardy.

No one else in the village, probably no one else in the county, owned any such tree, alive or dead. Dame Louisa's husband, who had been a sea-captain, had brought them from foreign parts. They were mere little twigs when they planted them on the first day of January, but they were full-grown and loaded with fruit by the next Christmas-day. Every Christmas they were cut down and sold, but they always grew again to their full height, in a year's time. They were not, it is true, the regulation Christmas-tree. That is they were not loaded with different and suitable gifts for every one in a family, as they stood there in Dame Louisa's yard. People always tied on those, after they had bought them, and had set them up in their own parlors. But these trees bore regular fruit like apple, or peach, or plum-trees, only there was a considerable

variety in it. These trees when in full fruitage were
festooned with strings of pop-corn, and weighed down
with apples and oranges and figs and bags of candy,
and it was really an amazing sight to see them out
there in Dame Louisa's front yard. But now they
were all yellow and dead, and not so much as one pop-
corn whitened the upper branches, neither was there
one candle shining out in the night. For the trees in
their prime had borne also little twinkling lights like
wax candles.

Dame Louisa looked out at her dead Christmas-
trees, and scowled. She could see the children out in
the road, and they were trudging along in the direction
of the White Woods. " Let 'em go," she snapped
to herself. " I guess they won't go far. I'll be rid of
their noise, any way."

She could hear poor Dame Penny's distressed voice
out in her yard, calling " Biddy, Biddy, Biddy ; " and
she scowled more fiercely than ever. " I'm glad she's
lost her old silver hen," she muttered to herself. She
had always suspected the silver hen of pecking at the
roots of the Christmas-trees and so causing them to
blast ; then, too, the silver hen had used to stand on
the fence and crow ; for, unlike other hens, she could
crow very beautifully, and that had disturbed her.

Dame Louisa had a very wise book, which she had
consulted to find the reason for the death of her
Christmas-trees, but all she could find in it was one

short item, which did not satisfy her at all. The book was on the plan of an encyclopædia, and she, having turned to the "ch's," found :

" Christmas-trees — very delicate when transplanted, especially sensitive, and liable to blast at any change in the moral atmosphere. Remedy: discover and confess the cause."

After reading this, Dame Louisa was always positive that Dame Penny's silver hen was at the root of the mischief, for she knew that she herself had never done anything to hurt the trees.

Dame Penny was so occupied in calling "Biddy, Biddy, Biddy," and shaking a little pan of corn, that she never noticed the children taking the road toward the White Woods. If she had done so she would have stopped them, for the White Woods was considered a very dangerous place. It was called white because it was always white even in midsummer. The trees and bushes, and all the undergrowth, every flower and blade of grass, were white with snow and frost all the year round, and all the learned men of the country had studied into the reason of it, and had come to the conclusion that the Woods lay in a direct draught from the North Pole and that produced the phenomenon. Nobody had penetrated very far into the White Woods, although many expeditions had been organized for that purpose. The cold was so terrible that it drove them back.

The children had heard all about the terrors of the White Woods. When they drew near it they took hold of one another's hands and snuggled as closely together as possible.

When they struck into the path at the entrance the intense cold turned their cheeks and noses blue in a moment, but they kept on, calling "Biddy, Biddy, Biddy!" in their shrill sweet trebles. Every twig on the trees was glittering white with hoar-frost, and all the dead blackberry-vines wore white wreaths, the bushes brushed the ground, they were so heavy with ice, and the air was full of fine white sparkles. The children's eyes were dazzled, but they kept on, stumbling through the icy vines and bushes, and calling "Biddy, Biddy, Biddy!"

It was quite late in the afternoon when they started, and pretty soon the sun went down and the moon arose, and that made it seem colder. It was like traveling through a forest of solid silver then, and every once in a while a little frozen clump of flowers would shine so that they would think it was the silver hen and dart forward, to find it was not.

About two hours after the moon arose, as they were creeping along, calling "Biddy, Biddy, Biddy!" more and more faintly, a singular, hoarse voice replied suddenly. "We don't keep any hens," said the voice, and all the children jumped and screamed, and looked about for the owner of it. He loomed up among some

bushes at their right. He was so dazzling white himself, and had such an indistinctness of outline, that
they had taken him for an oak-tree. But it was the
real Snow Man. They knew him in a moment, he
looked so much like his effigies that they used to make
in their yards.

"We don't keep any hens," repeated the Snow
Man. "What are you calling hens for in this
forest?"

The children huddled together as close as they could,
and the oldest boy explained: When he broke down
the oldest girl piped up and helped him.

"Well," said the Snow Man, "I haven't seen the
silver hen. I never did see any hens in these woods,
but she may be around here for all that. You had
better go home with me and spend the night. My
wife will be delighted to see you. We have never
had any company in our lives, and she is always scolding
about it."

The children looked at each other and shook harder
than they had done with cold.

"I'm — afraid our mothers — wouldn't — like to
have us," stammered the oldest boy.

"Nonsense," cried the Snow Man. "Here I have
been visiting you, time and time again, and stood whole
days out in your front yards, and you've never been
to see me. I think it is about time that I had some
return. Come along." With that the Snow Man

seized the right ear of the oldest boy between a finger and thumb, and danced him along, and all the rest, trembling, and whimpering under their breaths, followed.

It was not long before they reached the Snow Man's house, which was really quite magnificent: a castle built of blocks of ice fitted together like bricks, and with two splendid snow-lions keeping guard at the entrance. The Snow Man's wife stood in the door, and the Snow Children stood behind her and peeped around her skirts; they were smiling from ear to ear. They had never seen any company before, and they were so delighted that they did not know what to do.

THE SNOW MAN'S HOUSE.

"We have some company, wife," shouted the Snow Man.

"Bring them right in," said his wife with a beaming face. She was very handsome, with beautiful pink cheeks and blue eyes, and she wore a trailing white robe, like a queen. She kissed the children all around, and shivers crept down their backs, for it was like being kissed by an icicle. "Kiss your company, my dears," she said to the Snow Children, and they came bashfully forward and kissed Dame Penny's scholars with these same chilly kisses.

"Now," said the Snow Man's wife, "come right

in and sit down where it is cool — you look very hot."

"Hot," when the poor scholars were quite stiff with cold! They looked at one another in dismay, but did not dare say anything. They followed the Snow Man's wife into her grand parlor.

"Come right over here by the north window where it is cooler," said she, "and the children shall bring you some fans."

The Snow Children floated up with fans — all the Snow Man's family had a lovely floating gait — and the scholars took them with feeble curtesies, and began fanning. A stiff north wind blew in at the windows. The forest was all creaking and snapping with the cold. The poor children, fanning themselves, on an ice divan, would certainly have frozen if the Snow Man's wife had not suggested that they all have a little game of " puss-in-the-corner," to while away the time before dinner. That warmed them up a little, for they had to run very fast indeed to play with the Snow Children who seemed to fairly blow in the north wind from corner to corner.

But the Snow Man's wife stopped the play a little before dinner was announced ; she said the guests looked so warm that she was alarmed, and was afraid they might melt.

A whistle, that sounded just like the whistle of the north wind in the chimney, blew for dinner, and Dame

PUSS-IN-THE-CORNER.

Penny's scholars thought with delight that now they would have something warm. But every dish on the Snow Man's table was cold and frozen, and the Snow Man's wife kept urging them to eat this and that, because it was so nice and cooling, and they looked so warm.

After dinner they were colder than ever, even. Another game of "puss-in-the-corner" did not warm them much; they were glad when the Snow Man's wife suggested that they go to bed, for they had visions of warm blankets and comfortables. But when they were shown into the great north chamber, that was more like a hall than a chamber, with its walls of solid ice, its ice floor and its ice beds, their hearts sank. Not a blanket nor comfortable was to be seen; there were great silk bags stuffed with snow flakes instead of feathers on the beds, and that was all.

"If you are too warm in the night, and feel as if you were going to melt," said the Snow Man's wife, "you can open the south window and that will make a draught — there are none but the north windows open now."

The scholars curtesied and bade her good-night, and she kissed them and hoped they would sleep well. Then she trailed her splendid robe, which was decorated with real frost embroidery, down the ice stairs and left her guests to themselves. They were frantic with cold and terror, and the little ones began to cry.

They talked over the situation and agreed that they had better wait until the house was quiet and then run away. So they waited until they thought everybody must be asleep, and then cautiously stole toward the door. It was locked fast on the outside. The Snow Man's wife had slipped an icicle through the latch. Then they were in despair. It seemed as if they must freeze to death before morning. But it occurred to some of the older ones that they had heard their parents say that snow was really warm, and people had been kept warm and alive by burrowing under snow-drifts. And as there were enough snow-flake beds to use for coverlids also, they crept under them, having first shut the north windows, and were soon quite comfortable.

In the meantime there was a great panic in the village ; the children's parents were nearly wild. They came running to Dame Penny, but she was calling " Biddy, Biddy, Biddy ! " out in the moonlight, and knew nothing about them. Then they called outside Dame Louisa's window, but she pretended to be asleep, although she was really awake, and in a terrible panic.

She did not tell the parents how the children had gone to the White Woods, because she knew that they could not extricate them from the difficulty as well as she could herself. She knew all about the Snow Man and his wife, and how very anxious they were to have company.

So just as soon as the parents were gone and she heard their voices in the distance, she dressed herself, harnessed her old white horse into the great box-sleigh, got out all the tubs and pails that she had in the house, and went over to Dame Penny, who was still standing out in her front yard calling the silver hen and the children by turns.

"Come, Dame Penny," said Dame Louisa, "I want you to go with me to the White Woods and rescue the children. Bring out all the tubs and pails you have in the house, and we will pump them full of water."

TO THE RESCUE.

"The pails — full of water — what for?" gasped Dame Penny.

"To thaw them out," replied Dame Louisa; "they will very likely be wholly or partly frozen, and I have always heard that cold water was the only remedy to use."

Dame Penny said no more. She brought out all her tubs and pails, and they pumped them and Dame Louisa's full of water, and packed them into the sleigh — there were twelve of them. Then they climbed into the seat, slapped the reins over the back of the old white horse, and started off for the White Woods.

On the way Dame Louisa wept, and confessed what she had done to Dame Penny. "I have been a cross, selfish old woman," said she, "and I think that is the reason why my Christmas-trees were blasted. I don't believe your silver hen touched them."

She and Dame Penny called "Biddy, Biddy, Biddy!" and the names of the children, all the way. Dame Louisa drove straight to the Snow Man's house.

"They are more likely to be there than anywhere else, the Snow Man and his wife are so crazy to have company," said she.

When they arrived at the house, Dame Louisa left Dame Penny to hold the horse, and went in. The outer door was not locked and she wandered quite at her will, through the great ice saloons, and wind-swept corridors. When she came to the door with the icicle through the latch, she knew at once that the children were in that room, so she drew out the icicle and entered. The children were asleep, but she aroused them, and bade them be very quiet and follow her. They got out of the house without disturbing any of the family; but, once out, a new difficulty beset them. The children had been so nearly warm under their snow-flake beds that they began to freeze the minute the icy air struck them.

But Dame Louisa promptly seized them, while Dame Penny held the horse, and put them into the tubs and pails of water. Then she took hold of the horse's head, and backed him and turned around carefully, and they started off at full speed.

But it was not long before they discovered that they

were pursued. They heard the hoarse voice of the Snow Man behind them calling to them to stop.

"What are you taking away my company for?" shouted the Snow Man. "Stop, stop!"

The wind was at the back of the Snow Man, and he came with tremendous velocity. It was evident that he would soon overtake the old white horse who was stiff and somewhat lame. Dame Louisa whipped him up, but the Snow Man gained on them. The icy breath of the Snow Man blew over them. "Oh!" shrieked Dame Penny, "what shall we do, what shall we do?"

"Be quiet," said Dame Louisa with dignity. She untied her large poke-bonnet which was made of straw — she was unable to have a velvet one for winter, now her Christmas-trees were dead — and she hung it on the whip. Then she drew a match from her pocket, and set fire to the bonnet. The light fabric blazed up directly, and the Snow Man stopped short. "If you come any nearer," shrieked Dame Louisa, "I'll put this right in your face and — melt you!"

"Give me back my company," shouted the Snow Man in a doubtful voice.

"You can't have your company," said Dame Louisa, shaking the blazing bonnet defiantly at him.

"To think of the days I've spent in their yards, slowly melting and suffering everything, and my not having one visit back," grumbled the Snow Man.

But he stood still ; he never took a step forward after Dame Louisa had set her bonnet on fire.

It was lucky Dame Louisa had worn a worsted scarf tied over her bonnet, and could now use it for a bonnet.

The cold was intense, and had it not been that Dame Penny and Dame Louisa both wore their Bay State shawls over their beaver sacques, and their stone-marten tippets and muffs, and blue worsted stockings drawn over their shoes, they would certainly have frozen.   As for the children, they would never have reached home alive if it had not been for the pails and tubs of water.

"Do you feel as if you were thawing?" Dame Louisa asked the children after they had left the Snow Man behind.

" Yes, ma'am," said they.

Dame Louisa drove as fast as she could, with thankful tears running down her cheeks.   "I've been a wicked, cross old woman," said she again and again, " and that is what blasted my Christmas-trees."

It was the dawn of Christmas-day when they came in sight of Dame Louisa's house.

"Oh ! what is that twinkling out in the yard?" cried the children.

They could all see little fairy-like lights twinkling out in Dame Louisa's yard.

" It looks just as the Christmas-trees used to," said Dame Penny.

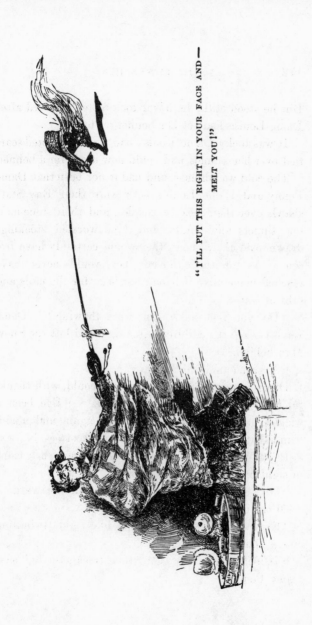

"I'LL PUT THIS RIGHT IN YOUR FACE AND — MELT YOU!"

" Oh ! I can't believe it," cried Dame Louisa, her heart beating wildly.

But when they came opposite the yard, they saw that it was true. Dame Louisa's Christmas-trees stood there all twinkling with lights, and covered with trailing garlands of pop-corn, oranges, apples, and candy-bags ; their yellow branches had turned green and the Christmas-trees were in full glory.

" Oh ! what is that shining so out in Dame Penny's yard ? " cried the children, who were entirely thawed, and only needed to get home to their parents and have some warm breakfast, and Christmas-presents, to be quite themselves. " Biddy, Biddy, Biddy ! " cried Dame Penny, and Dame Louisa and the children chimed in, calling, " Biddy, Biddy, Biddy ! "

It was indeed the silver hen, and following her were twelve little silver chickens. She had stolen a nest in Dame Louisa's barn and nobody had known it until she appeared on Christmas morning with her brood of silver chickens.

" Every scholar shall have one of the silver chickens for a Christmas present," said Dame Penny.

" And each shall have one of my Christmas-trees," said Dame Louisa.

Then all the scholars cried out with delight, the Christmas-bells in the village began to ring, the silver hen flew up on the fence and crowed, the sun shone broadly out, and it was a merry Christmas-day.

TOBY.

Aunt Malvina was sitting at the window watching for a horse-car which she wanted to take. Uncle Jack was near the register in a comfortable easy chair, his feet on an embroidered foot-rest, and Letitia, just as close to him as she could get her little rocking-chair, was sewing her square of patchwork " over and over." Letitia had to sew a square of patchwork " over and over " every day.

Aunt Malvina, who was not uncle Jack's wife, as one might suspect, but his elder sister, was a very small, frisky little lady, with a thin, rosy face, and a little bobbing bunch of gray curls on each side of it. She talked very fast, and she talked all the time, so she accomplished a vast deal of talking in the course of a day, and the people she happened to be with did a vast deal of listening.

She was talking now, and uncle Jack was listening, with his head leaning comfortably against a pretty tidy all over daisies in Kensington work, and so was Letitia, taking cautious little stitches in her patchwork.

" Mrs. Welcome," aunt Malvina had just remarked,

"has got a little colored boy as black as Toby to wait on table."

Letitia opened her sober, light gray eyes very wide, and stared reflectively at aunt Malvina.

"It was dark as Pokonoket when we came out of church last night," said aunt Malvina after a time, in the course of conversation.

Letitia stared reflectively at her again.

"There's my car coming around the corner!" cried aunt Malvina, and ran friskily out of the room. Just outside the door she turned and thrust her face, with the little gray curls dancing around it, in again for a last word. "O, Jack!" cried she, "I hear that Edward Simonds' eldest son is as crazy as a loon!"

"Is?"

"Yes; isn't it dreadful? Good-by!" Aunt Malvina frisked airily downstairs, and out on the street, barely in time to secure her car.

When Letitia heard the front door close after her, she quilted her needle carefully into her square, then she folded the patchwork up neatly, rose, and laid it together with her thimble, scissors, and cotton, in her little rocking-chair. Then she went and stood still before uncle Jack, with her arms folded. It was a way she had when she wanted information. People rather smiled to see Letitia sometimes, but uncle Jack had always encouraged her in it; he said it was quaint. Letitia's face was very sober, and very innocent, and very round, and her hair was very long and light, and hung in two smooth braids, with a neat blue bow on the end of each, down her back.

LETITIA STOOD BEFORE UNCLE JACK.

Uncle Jack gazed inquiringly at her through his half-closed eyes. "What is it, Letitia?"

"Aunt Malvina said 'as black as Toby,'" said

Letitia with a look half of inquiry, half of anxious abstraction. What Letitia could find out herself she never asked other people.

"Yes ; I know she did," replied uncle Jack.

" Then she said, ' Dark as Pokonoket.' "

" Yes ; she said that too."

" And then she said, ' Crazy as a loon.' "

" Yes ; she did."

" Uncle Jack, what is Toby, and what is Pokonoket, and what is a loon ? "

" Toby," said uncle Jack slowly and impressively, " lives in Pokonoket, and keeps a loon."

" Oh ! " said Letitia, in a tone which implied that she was both relieved and amazed at her own stupidity.

" Yes ; perhaps you would like to hear something more particular about Toby — how he got married, for instance ? "

" I should, very much indeed," replied Letitia gravely and promptly.

" Well, you had better sit down ; it will take a few minutes to tell it."

Letitia carefully took her patchwork, her thimble, her spool of cotton, and her scissors out of her little rocking-chair and laid them on the table ; then she sat down, and crossed her hands in her lap.

" Now, if you are ready," said uncle Jack, laughing a little to himself as he looked down at her. Then he related as follows : " Toby is a little black fellow, not much taller than you are, and he lives in Pokono-ket, and keeps a loon. Toby's hair is very short and kinky, and his mouth is wide, and always curves up a little at the corners, as if he were laughing ; his eyes are astonishingly bright; but all the people's eyes are bright in Pokonoket.

"Pokonoket is a very dark country. It always was dark. The most ancient historians make no mention of its ever being light in Pokonoket.

"The cause of the darkness has never been exactly understood. Philosophers and men of science have worked very hard over it, but all the conclusion they have been able to arrive at is, it must be due to fog, or smoke, or atmospheric phenomena. The most celebrated of them are in favor of atmospheric phenomena, and they are probably correct.

"The houses are always furnished with lamps, of course, and everybody carries a lantern. No one dreams of stirring out in Pokonoket without a lantern. The men go to their work with lanterns, the ladies take theirs when they go out shopping, and all the children have their little lanterns to carry to school.

"On account of the darkness, there are some very curious customs in Pokonoket. One is, all the inhabitants are required by law to wear squeaky shoes. Whenever anybody's shoes don't squeak according to the prescribed standard he is fined, and sometimes even imprisoned, if he persists in his offense. A great

SCHOOL. CHILDREN IN POKONOKET.

many sad accidents are prevented by this custom. People hear each other's shoes squeaking in the darkness at quite a distance, and don't run into each other. Pokonoket shoemakers make a specialty of squeaky shoes, and the squeakier they are, the higher prices they bring; they can even put in new squeaks when the old ones are worn out. It is a very common thing to see a Pokonoket man with his little boy's shoes under his arm, carrying them to a shoemaker to get them re-squeaked.

"Another funny custom is the wearing of phosphorescent buttons. Everybody, men, women and children, are required to wear phosphorescent buttons on their outside garments. They are quite large — about the size of an old-fashioned cent — and there are, generally, two rows of them down the front of a garment. It is rather a frightful sight to see a person with phosphorescent buttons on his coat advancing toward one in the dark, till you are accustomed to it; he looks as if he had two rows of enormous eyes.

"Then, when the weather is stormy, everybody has to carry an umbrella with his name on it in phosphorescent letters. In this way, nobody's eyes are put out, and no umbrellas are lost. Otherwise, umbrellas would get so hopelessly mixed up in a dark country like Pokonoket that it would require a special sitting of Parliament to sort them out again.

"It may seem rather odd that they should, but the

inhabitants of Pokonoket are, as a general thing, very much attached to their country, and could not be hired to leave it for any other. It is a very peaceful place. There are no jails, and no criminals are executed in its bounds. If occasionally a person commits a crime that would merit such extreme punishment, he puts out his lantern, and rips off his phosphorescent buttons, and nobody can find him to punish.

" But commonly, folks in Pokonoket do not commit great crimes, and are a very peaceful, industrious and happy people.

" They have never had any wars amongst themselves, and their country has never been invaded by a foreign foe ; all that they ever have had to seriously threaten their peace and safety was the Ogress.

" A terrible ogress once lived in Pokonoket, and devoured everybody she could catch. Nobody knew when his life was safe, and the worst of it was, they did not know where she lived, or they would have gone in a body and disposed of her. She had a habitation somewhere in the darkness, but nobody knew where — it might be right in their midst. There are a great many inconveniences about a dark country.

" Well, Toby who kept the loon, lived in a little hut on one of the principal streets. He was a widower, and lived with his six grandchildren who were all quite small and went to school. They were his daughter's children. She had died a few years before of a

POKONOKET IN STORMY WEATHER.

disease quite common in Pokonoket, and almost always fatal. It had a long name which the doctors had given it, which really meant, ' wanting light.'

" Toby was rather feeble and rheumatic, and it was about all he could do to knit stockings for his grand-children, and make soup for their dinner. Almost all day, except when he was stirring the soup, which he made in a great kettle set into a brick oven, he was sitting on a little stool in his doorway, knitting, and the loon sat on a perch at his right hand. The loon who was a very large bird, was crazy, and thought he was a bobolink. *Link, link, bobolink!* he sang all day long, instead of crying in the way a loon usually does. His voice was not anywhere near the right pitch for a bobolink's song, but that made no dif-ference. *Link, link, bobolink!* he kept on singing from morning till night.

" Toby did not mind knitting, but he did not like to make the soup. It had never seemed to him to be a man's work, and besides, it hurt his old, rheumatic back to bend over the soup-kettle. That was what put it into his head to get married again. He thought if he could find a pleasant, tidy woman, who would stir the soup while he sat in the door beside the loon, and knit the stockings, he could live much more comfortably than he did.

" Now Toby thought he knew of just the one he wanted. She was a widow who lived a few squares from him. She was as sweet-tempered as a dove, and nobody could find a speck of dirt in her house if he was to search all day with a lantern.

TOBY AND THE CRAZY LOON.

"Toby thought about it for a long time. He did not wish to take any rash step, but his back got lamer and stiffer, and when one day the soup burned on to the kettle, and he dropped some stitches in his stocking running to lift it off, he made up his mind.

" The very next morning after his six grandchildren had gone to school, he put on his coat with phosphorescent buttons, lit his lantern, and started out. *Link, link, bobolink!* cried the crazy loon as he went out the door.

" ' Yes ; I am going to bring home a pleasant and neat mistress for you, and maybe you will recover your reason,' said Toby.

" *Link, link, bobolink!* cried the crazy loon.

" Toby limped away through the darkness. The wind was blowing hard that morning, and as he turned the corner, puff ! came a gust and blew out his lantern.

" He felt in every pocket, but he had not a match in one of them. He hesitated whether to go back for one or not. Finally, he thought he knew the way pretty well and would risk it. His back was worse than ever that morning, and he did not want to take any unnecessary steps. So he fumbled along until he came to the street where the widow's home was ; there were five more just like hers, and they stood in a row together.

" Much to Toby's dismay, there was not a light in either.

" ' Well,' he reflected, ' she is prudent, and is saving her oil, I dare say, and I can inquire.'

" So he felt his way along to the first house in the row — he could just see them looming up in the darkness. He poked his head inside the door. ' Mrs. Clover-leaf ! ' cried he, ' are you in there? My lantern has gone out, and I cannot tell which is your house.'

" There came a little grunt in reply.

" ' Mrs. Clover-leaf ! ' cried Toby again.

" ' I am here; what do you want?' answered a voice in the darkness.

" It was so sharp that Toby felt for a moment as if his ears were being sawed off, and he clapped his hands on them involuntarily. ' Bless me ! I had forgotten that Mrs. Clover-leaf had such a voice,' thought he.

" ' What do you want ? ' said the voice again.

" It did not sound quite so sharp this time. He had become a little used to it, and, after all, a sharp voice would not prevent her being neat and pleasant and stirring the soup carefully.

" So he said, as sweetly and coaxingly as he was able, ' I have come to see if you would like to marry me, Mrs. Clover-leaf.'

" ' I don't know,' said the sharp voice, ' I had not thought of changing my condition.'

" ' All you would have to do,' said Toby pleadingly, ' would be to stir the soup for my grandchildren's dinner, while I knit the stockings.'

" There came a sound like the smacking of lips out

of the darkness within the house.   'Oh! you have grandchildren; I forgot,' said the voice; 'how many?'

"'Six,' replied Toby.

"'I shall be pleased to marry you,' cried the voice; and Toby heard the squeaking of shoes, as if the widow were coming.

"'When shall we be married?' said the sharp voice right in Toby's ear.

"He jumped so that he could not answer for a minute. 'Well,' said he finally — 'I don't want to hurry you, Mrs. Clover-leaf, but the soup is to be made for dinner, and if I don't finish the pair of stockings I am on to-day, my eldest grandchild will have to go barefoot. A pair of stockings only lasts one a week.' And Toby sighed so pitifully that it ought to have touched any widow's heart.

"The widow laughed. Toby felt rather hurt that she should. He did not know of any joke. It was a curious kind of a laugh, too; as bad in its way as her voice. But what she said the next minute set matters right.

"'Let us go and get married, then,' said she, 'and I will go right home and make the soup, and you can finish the stocking.'

"Toby was delighted. 'Thank you, my dear Mrs. Clover-leaf!' he cried, and offered her his arm gallantly, and they set off together to the minister's.

"The widow took such enormous strides that Toby

had to run to keep up with her. She was much taller than he, and her bonnet was very large, and almost hid her face. Toby could hardly have seen her, if he had had his lantern; still he could not help wishing that one of them had one, but the widow said her oil was out, so there was no help for it.

"Once or twice when she turned her head toward him, Toby thought her eyes looked about twice as large and bright as phosphorescent buttons, and he felt a little startled, but he told himself that it was only his imagination, of course.

"When they reached the minister's, there was no light in his house, either, and it occurred to Toby that it was Fast Day. Once a week, Pokonoket ministers sit in total darkness all day, and eat nothing.

"When Toby called, the minister poked his head out of the study window, and asked what he wanted.

"Toby told him, and he and the widow stood in front of the study window, and were married in the dark, and Toby gave a phosphorescent button for the fee.

"The widow took longer steps than ever on the way home, and Toby ran till he was all out of breath; she fairly lifted him off his feet sometimes, and carried him along on her arm.

"*Link, link, bobolink!* sang the crazy loon when Toby and his bride entered the house.

"'Now let's have a light,' cried Toby's wife, and her voice was sharper than ever. It frightened the

crazy loon so that he left the link off the end of his
song, and merely said bobo —

"'Yes,' answered Toby, bustling about cheerfully

TOBY RAN TILL HE WAS OUT OF BREATH.

after the matches, 'and then you will make the soup.'

"'I will make the soup,' laughed his wife.

"Toby felt frightened, he hardly knew why, but he

found the matches, and lit the lamp. Then he turned to look at his new wife, and saw — the Ogress! He had married the Ogress! Horrors!

" Toby sank down on his knees and shook with fear, his little kinky curls bristling up all over his head.

" 'Pshaw!' said the Ogress contemptuously. 'You needn't shake! Do you suppose I would eat such a little tough, bony fellow as you for supper? No! When do your grandchildren come home from school?'

" 'Oh,' groaned Toby, 'take me, dear Mrs. Ogress, and spare my grandchildren!'

" 'I should smile,' said the Ogress. That was all the reply she made. She talked popular slang along with her other bad habits.

" Toby wept, and groaned, and pleaded, but he could not get another word out of her. She filled the great soup-kettle with water, set it over the fire (Toby shuddered to see her), then she sat down to wait for the grandchildren to come home from school. She was uncommonly homely, even for an ogress, and she wore a brown calico dress that was very unbecoming.

" Poor Toby gazed at her in fear and disgust. He looked out of the door, expecting every moment to see his grandchildren coming, one behind the other, swinging their little lanterns. School children always walked one behind the other in Pokonoket. It was against the law to walk two abreast.

" Finally, when the Ogress was leaning over the

soup-kettle, putting her fingers in, to see if it was hot enough, Toby slipped out of the door, and ran straight to the minister's.

"He stood outside the study window and groaned.

"'What is the trouble?' asked the minister, poking his head out.

"'Oh,' cried Toby, 'you married me to the — ¬ress!'

You don't say so!' cried the minister.

'Yes, I do! What shall I do? She is waiting or my grandchildren, and the soup-kettle is on!'

"'Wait a minute,' said the minister. 'In a matter of life and death, it is permitted to light a lamp on a Fast Day. This is a matter of life and death; so I will light a lamp and look in my Encyclopædia of Useful Knowledge.'

"So the minister lit his lamp, and took his Encyclopædia of Useful Knowledge from the study shelf.

"He turned over the leaves till he came to Ogre; then he found Ogress, and read all there was under that head.

"'H'm!' he said; 'h'm, h'm! An Ogress is an inconceivably hideous creature, yet, like all females, she is inordinately vain, and is extremely susceptible to any insinuations against her personal appearance! H'm!' said the minister; 'h'm, h'm! I know what I will do.'

"Now it was one of the laws in Pokonoket that

nobody should have a looking-glass but the minister. Once a year the ladies of his congregation were allowed to look at themselves in it; that was all. I do not know the reason for this law, but it existed.

"The minister took his looking-glass under his arm, and came out of his house. 'Now, Toby,' said he, 'take me home with you.'

" 'But I am afraid she will eat you, sir,' said Toby doubtfully. 'You are not as thin as I am.'

" 'I am not in the least afraid,' replied the minister cheerfully.

"So Toby took heart a little, and hastened home with the minister.

"*Link, link, bobolink!* cried the crazy loon as they went in the door.

"The minister walked straight up to the Ogress, who was standing beside the soup-kettle, and held the looking-glass before her.

"When she saw her face in all its hideous ugliness, the shock was so great, for she had always thought herself very handsome, that she gave one shriek and fell down quite dead."

Letitia gave a sigh of relief, and uncle Jack yawned. "Well, Letitia, that's all," said he, "only Toby married the real widow, Mrs. Clover-leaf, the next day, and she made the soup to perfection, and he had nothing to do all the rest of his life, but to sit in the doorway beside the crazy loon, and knit stockings for his grandchildren."

"Thank you, uncle Jack," said Letitia gravely. Then she got her square of patchwork off the table and sat down and finished sewing it over and over.

THE PATCHWORK SCHOOL.

Once upon a time there was a city which possessed
a very celebrated institution for the reformation of un-
ruly children. It was, strictly speaking, a Reform
School, but of a very peculiar kind.

It had been established years before by a benevolent
lady, who had a great deal of money, and wished to
do good with it. After thinking a long time, she had
hit upon this plan of founding a school for the improvement of children who tried their parents and all
their friends by their ill behavior. More especially
was it designed for ungrateful and discontented children ; indeed it was mainly composed of this last class.

There was a special set of police in the city, whose
whole duty was to keep a sharp lookout for ill-natured
fretting children, who complained of their parents' treatment, and thought other boys and girls were much better
off than they, and to march them away to the school.
These police all wore white top boots, tall peaked hats,
and carried sticks with blue ribbon bows on them, and
were very readily distinguished. Many a little boy
on his way to school has dodged round a corner to
avoid one, because he had just been telling his mother

that another little boy's mother gave him twice as much pie for dinner as he had. He wouldn't breathe easy till he had left the white top boots out of sight; and he would tremble all day at every knock on the door.

There was not a child in the city but had a great horror of this school, though it may seem rather strange that they should; for the punishment, at first thought, did not seem so very terrible. Ever since it was established, the school had been in charge of a very singular little old woman. Nobody had ever known where she came from. The benevolent lady who founded the institution, had brought her to the door one morning in her coach, and the neighbors had seen the little brown, wizened creature, with a most extraordinary gown on, alight and enter. This was all any one had ever known about her. In fact, the benevolent lady had come upon her in the course of her travels in a little German town, sitting in a garret window, behind a little box-garden of violets, sewing patchwork. After that, she became acquainted with her, and finally hired her to superintend her school. You see, the benevolent lady had a very tender heart, and though she wanted to reform the naughty children of her native city, and have them grow up to be good men and women, she did not want them to be shaken, nor have their ears cuffed; so the ideas advanced by the strange little old woman just suited her.

"Set 'em to sewing patchwork," said this little old woman, sewing patchwork vigorously herself as she spoke. She was dressed in a gown of bright-colored patchwork, with a patchwork shawl over her shoulders. Her cap was made of tiny squares of patchwork, too. "If they are sewing patchwork," went on the little old woman, "they can't be in mischief. Just make 'em sit in little chairs and sew patchwork, boys and girls alike. Make 'em sit and sew patchwork, when the bees are flying over the clover, out in the bright sunlight, and the great blue-winged butterflies stop with the roses just outside the windows, and the robins are singing in the cherry-trees, and they'll turn over a new leaf, you'll see!" sewing away with a will.

THE PATCHWORK WOMAN.

So the school was founded, the strange little old woman placed over it, and it really worked admirably. It was the pride of the city. Strangers who visited it were always taken to visit the Patchwork School, for that was the name it went by. There sat the children, in their little chairs, sewing patchwork. They were dressed in little patchwork uniforms ; the girls wore blue and white patchwork frocks and pink and white patchwork pinafores, and the boys blue and white patchwork trousers, with pinafores like the girls. Their cheeks were round and rosy, for they had plenty to eat — bread and milk three times a day — but they looked sad, and tears were standing in the corners of a good many eyes. How could they help it ? It did seem as if the loveliest roses in the whole country were blossoming in the garden of the Patchwork School, and there were swarms of humming-birds flying over them, and great red and blue-winged butterflies. And there were tall cherry-trees a little way from the window, and they used to be perfectly crimson with fruit ; and the way the robins would sing in them ! Later in the season there were apple and peach-trees, too, the apples and great rosy peaches fairly dragging the branches to the ground, and all in sight from the window of the schoolroom.

No wonder the poor little culprits cooped up indoors sewing red and blue and green pieces of calico together, looked sad. Every day bales of calico were left at the door of the Patchwork School, and it all had to be cut up in little bits and sewed together again. When the children heard the heavy tread of the porters bringing in the bales of new calico, the tears would leave the corners of their eyes and trickle down their poor little cheeks, at the prospect of the additional work they would have to do. All the patchwork had to be sewed over and over, and every crooked or too long stitch had to be picked out; for the Patch-work Woman was very par-ticular. They had to make all their own clothes of patch-work, and after those were done, patchwork bed quilts, which were given to the city poor; so the benevolent lady killed two birds with one stone, as you might say.

THE PATCHWORK GIRL.

Of course, children staid in the Patchwork School differ-ent lengths of time, according to their different of-fenses. But there were very few children in the city who had not sat in a little chair and sewed patch-work, at one time or another, for a greater or less period. Sooner or later, the best children were sure to think they were ill-treated by their parents, and had to go to bed earlier than they ought, or did not have as much candy as other children ; and the police would hear them grumbling, and drag them off to the Patch-work School. The Mayor's son, especially, who might be supposed to fare as well as any little boy

in the city, had been in the school any number of
times.

There was one little boy in the city, however, whom
the white-booted police had not yet found any occasion
to arrest, though one might have thought he had more
reason than a good many others to complain of his lot
in life. In the first place, he had a girl's name, and
any one knows that would be a great cross to a boy.
His name was Julia ; his parents had called him so
on account of his having a maiden aunt who had
promised to leave her money to him if he was named
for her.

So there was no help for it, but it was a great trial
to him, for the other boys plagued him unmercifully,
and called him " missy," and " sissy," and said " she "
instead of " he " when they were speaking of him.
Still he never complained to his parents, and told them
he wished they had called him some other name. His
parents were very poor, hard-working people, and Julia
had much coarser clothes than the other boys, and
plainer food, but he was always cheerful about it, and
never seemed to think it at all hard that he could not
have a velvet coat like the Mayor's son, or carry cakes
for lunch to school like the lawyer's little boy.

But perhaps the greatest cross which Julia had to bear,
and the one from which he stood in the greatest danger of
getting into the Patchwork School, was his Grandmothers. I don't mean to say that grandmothers are

to be considered usually as crosses.   A dear old lady
seated with her knitting beside the fire, is a pleasant
person to have in the house.   But Julia had four, and
he had to hunt for their spectacles, and pick up their
balls of yarn so much that he got very little time to
play.   It was an unusual thing, but the families on
both sides were very long-lived, and there actually
were four grandmothers ;   two great ones, and two common ones ;   two on each side of the fireplace, with their
knitting work, in Julia's home.   They were nice old
ladies, and Julia loved them dearly, but they lost their
spectacles all the time, and were always dropping their
balls of yarn, and it did make a deal of work for
one boy to do.   He could have hunted up spectacles
for one Grandmother, but when it came to four, and
one was always losing hers while he was finding
another's, and one ball of yarn would drop and roll
off, while he was picking up another — well, it was
really bewildering at times.   Then he had to hold the
skeins of yarn for them to wind, and his arms used to
ache, and he could hear the boys shouting at a game
of ball outdoors, maybe.   But he never refused to do
anything his Grandmothers asked him to, and did it
pleasantly, too ; and it was not on that account he got
into the Patchwork School.

It was on Christmas day that Julia was arrested and
led away to the Patchwork School.   It happened in
this way : As I said before, Julia's parents were poor,

JULIA WAS ARRESTED ON CHRISTMAS DAY.

and it was all they could do to procure the bare com-
forts of life for their family ; there was very little to
spend for knickknacks. But I don't think Julia would
have complained at that ; he would have liked useful
articles just as well for Christmas presents, and would
not have been unhappy because he did not find some
useless toy in his stocking, instead of some article
of clothing, which he needed to make him comfortable.

But he had had the same things over and over, over
and over, Christmas after Christmas. Every year
each of his Grandmothers knit him two pairs of blue
woollen yarn stockings, and hung them for him on
Christmas Eve, for a Christmas present. There they
would hang — eight pairs of stockings with nothing in
them, in a row on the mantel shelf, every Christmas
morning.

Every year Julia thought about it for weeks before
Christmas, and hoped and hoped he would have something different this time, but there they always hung,
and he had to go and kiss his Grandmothers, and pre-
tend he liked the stockings the best of anything he could
have had ; for he would not have hurt their feelings for
the world.

His parents might have bettered matters a little, but
they did not wish to cross the old ladies either, and
they had to buy so much yarn they could not afford to
get anything else.

The worst of it was, the stockings were knit so well,

and of such stout material, that they never wore out, so Julia never really needed the new ones ; if he had, that might have reconciled him to the sameness of his Christmas presents, for he was a very sensible boy. But his bureau drawers were full of the blue stockings rolled up in neat little hard balls — all the balls he ever had; the tears used to spring up in his eyes every time he looked at them.   But he never said a word till the Christmas when he was twelve years old.   Somehow that time he was unusually cast down at the sight of the eight pairs of stockings hanging in a row under the mantel shelf ; but he kissed and thanked his Grand- mothers just as he always had.

When he was out on the street a little later, how- ever, he sat down in a doorway and cried.   He could not help it.   Some of the other boys had such lovely presents, and he had nothing but these same blue woollen stockings.

" What's the matter, little boy ? " asked a voice.

Without looking up, Julia sobbed out his troubles ; but what was his horror when he felt himself seized by the arm and lifted up, and found that he was in the grasp of a policeman in white top boots.   The police- man did not mind Julia's tears and entreaties in the least, but led him away to the Patchwork School, wav- ing his stick with its blue ribbon bow as majestically as a drum major.

So Julia had to sit down in a little chair, and sew

patchwork with the rest.   He did not mind the close work as much as some of the others, for he was used to being kept indoors, attending to his Grandmothers' wants ; but he disliked to sew.   His term of punishment was a long one.   The Patchwork Woman, who fixed it, thought it looked very badly for a little boy to be complaining because his kind grandparents had given him some warm stockings instead of foolish toys.

The first thing the children had to do when they entered the school, was to make their patchwork clothes, as I have said.   Julia had got his finished and was busily sewing on a red and green patchwork quilt, in a tea-chest pattern, when, one day, the Mayor came to visit the school.   Just then his son did not happen to be serving a term there; the Mayor never visited it with visitors of distinction when he was.

To-day he had a Chinese Ambassador with him. The Patchwork Woman sat behind her desk on the platform and sewed patchwork, the Mayor in his fine broadcloth sat one side of her, and the Chinese Ambassador, in his yellow satin gown, on the other.

The Ambassador's name was To-Chum.   The children could not help stealing glances occasionally at his high eyebrows and braided queue, but they cast their eyes on their sewing again directly.

The Mayor and the Ambassador staid about an hour; then after they had both made some remarks —

the Ambassador made his in Chinese; he could speak English, but his remarks in Chinese were wiser — they rose to go.

Now, the door of the Patchwork School was of a very peculiar structure. It was made of iron of a great thickness, and opened like any safe door, only it had more magic about it than any safe door ever had. At a certain hour in the afternoon, it shut of its own accord, and opened at a certain hour in the morning, when the Patchwork Woman repeated a formula before it. The formula did no good whatever at any other time; the door was so constructed that not even its inventor could open it after it shut at the certain hour of the afternoon, before the certain hour the next morning.

Now the Mayor and the Chinese Ambassador had staid rather longer than they should have. They had been so interested in the school that they had not noticed how the time was going, and the Patchwork Woman had been so taken up with a very intricate new pattern that she failed to remind them, as was her custom.

So it happened that while the Mayor got through the iron door safely, just as the Chinese Ambassador was following it suddenly swung to, and shut in his braided queue at a very high point.

Then there was the Ambassador on one side of the door, and his queue on the other, and the door could

JULIA ENTERTAINS THE AMBASSADOR THROUGH THE KEYHOLE

not possibly be opened before morning.   Here was a
terrible dilemma ! What was to be done? There
stood the children, their patchwork in their hands,
staring, open-mouthed, at the queue dangling through
the door, and the Patchwork Woman pale with dismay,
in their midst, on one side of the door, and on the
other side was the terror-stricken Mayor, and the poor
Chinese Ambassador.

"Can't anything be done?" shouted the Mayor
through the keyhole — there was a very large keyhole.

"No," the Patchwork Woman said.   "The door
won't open till six o'clock to-morrow morning."

"Oh, try ! " groaned the Mayor.   "Say the
formula."

She said the formula, to satisfy them, but the door
staid firmly shut.   Evidently the Chinese Ambassador
would have to stay where he was until morning, unless
he had the Mayor snip his queue off, which was not to
be thought of.

So the Mayor, who was something of a philosopher,
set about accommodating himself, or rather his friend,
to the situation.

"It is inevitable," said he to the Ambassador.   "I
am very sorry, but everybody has to conform to the
customs of the institutions of the countries which they
visit.   I will go and get you some dinner, and an
extra coat.   I will keep you company through the
night, and morning will come before you know it."

" Well," sighed the Chinese Ambassador, standing on tiptoe so his queue should not pull so hard. He was a patient man, but after he had eaten his dinner the time seemed terrible long.

" Why don't you talk? " said he to the Mayor, who was dozing beside him in an easy-chair. " Can't you tell me a story? "

" I never did such a thing in my life," replied the Mayor, rousing himself; " but I am very sorry for you, dear sir; perhaps the Patchwork Woman can."

So he asked the Patchwork Woman through the keyhole.

" I never told a story in my life," said she; " but there's a boy here that I heard telling a beautiful one the other day. Here, Julia," called she, " come and tell a story to the Chinese Ambassador."

Julia really knew a great many stories which his Grandmothers had taught him, and he sat on a little stool and told them through the keyhole all night to the Chinese Ambassador.

He and the Mayor were so interested that morning came and the door swung open before they knew it. The poor Ambassador drew a long breath, and put his hand around to his queue to see if it was safe. Then he wanted to thank and reward the boy who had made the long night hours pass so pleasantly.

" What is he in here for? " asked the Mayor, patting Julia, who could hardly keep his eyes open.

THE GRANDMOTHERS ENJOY THE CHINESE TOYS.

"He grumbled about his Christmas presents," replied the Patchwork Woman.

"What did you have?" inquired the Mayor.

"Eight pairs of blue yarn stockings," answered Julia, rubbing his eyes.

"And the year before?"

"Eight pairs of blue yarn stockings."

"And the year before that?"

"Eight pairs of blue yarn stockings."

"Didn't you ever have anything for Christmas presents but blue yarn stockings?" asked the astonished Mayor.

"No, sir," said Julia meekly.

Then the whole story came out. Julia, by dint of questioning, told some, and the other children told the rest; and finally, in the afternoon, orders came to dress him in his own clothes, and send him home. But when he got there, the Mayor and Chinese Ambassador had been there before him, and there hung the eight pairs of blue yarn stockings under the mantel-shelf, crammed full of the most beautiful things — knives, balls, candy — everything he had ever wanted, and the mantel-shelf piled high also.

A great many of the presents were of Chinese manufacture; for the Ambassador considered them, of course, superior, and he wished to express his gratitude to Julia as forcibly as he could. There was one stocking entirely filled with curious Chinese tops. A little round head, so much like the Ambassador's that it actually startled Julia, peeped out of the stocking. But it was only a top in the shape of a little man in a yellow silk gown, who could spin around very successfully on one foot, for an astonishing length of time. There was a Chinese lady-top too, who fanned herself coquettishly as she spun ; and a mandarin who nodded wisely. The tops were enough to turn a boy's head.

There were equally curious things in the other stockings. Some of them Julia had no use for, such as silk for dresses, China crape shawls and fans, but they were just the things for his Grandmothers, who, after this, sat beside the fireplace, very prim and fine, in stiff silk gowns, with China crape shawls over their shoulders, and Chinese fans in their hands, and queer shoes on their feet. Julia liked their presents just as well as he did his own, and probably the Ambassador knew that he would.

The Mayor had filled one stocking himself with bonbons, and Julia picked out all the peppermints amongst them for his Grandmothers. They were very fond of peppermints. Then he went to work to find their spectacles, which had been lost ever since he had been away.

THE SQUIRE'S SIXPENCE.

PATIENCE MATHER was saying the seven-multipli-
cation table, when she heard a heavy step in the entry.

"That is Squire Bean," whispered her friend,
Martha Joy, who stood at her elbow.

Patience stopped short in horror. Her especial
bugbear in mathematics was eight-times-seven; she
was coming toward it fast—could she remember it,
with old Squire Bean looking at her?

"Go on," said the teacher severely. She was quite
young, and also stood in some awe of Squire Bean,
but she did not wish her pupils to discover it, so she
pretended to ignore that step in the entry. Squire
Bean walked with a heavy gilt-headed cane which
always went clump, clump, at every step; beside he
shuffled — one could always tell who was coming.

"Seven times seven," begun Patience trembling —
then the door opened — there stood Squire Bean.

The teacher rose promptly. She tried to be very
easy and natural, but her pretty round cheeks turned
red and white by turns.

"Good-morning, Squire Bean," said she. Then
she placed a chair on the platform for him.

" *Good*-morning," said he, and seated himself in a lumbering way — he was rather stiff with rheumatism. He was a large old man in a green camlet cloak with brass buttons.

"You may go on with the exercises," said he to the teacher, after he had adjusted himself and wiped his face solemnly with a great red handkerchief.

"Go on, Patience," said the teacher.

So Patience piped up in her little weak soprano : "Seven times seven are forty-nine. Eight times seven are " — She stopped short. Then she begun over again — " Eight times seven " —

The class with toes on the crack all swayed forward to look at her, the pupils at the foot stepped off till they swung it into a half-circle. Hands came up and gyrated wildly.

"Back on the line !" said the teacher sternly. Then they stepped back, but the hands indicative of superior knowledge still waved, the coarse jacket-sleeves and the gingham apron-sleeves slipping back from the thin childish wrists.

" Eight times seven are eighty-nine," declared Patience desperately. The hands shook frantically, some of the owners stepped off the line again in their eagerness.

Patience's cheeks were red as poppies, her eyes were full of tears.

"You may try once more, Patience," said the

teacher, who was distressed herself. She feared lest
Squire Bean might think that it was her fault, and
that she was not a competent teacher, because Patience
Mather did not know eight-times-seven.

So Patience started again — " Eight times seven " —
She paused for a mighty
mental effort — she must get
it right this time. " Six " —
she began feebly.

" What! " said S q u i r e
Bean suddenly, in a deep
voice which sounded like a
growl.

Then all at once poor little Patience heard a whisper
sweet as an angel's in her
ear : " Fifty-six."

" Eight times seven are
fifty-six," said she convul-
sively.

" Right," said the teacher
with a relieved look. The
hands went down. Patience
stood with her neat little

" SIX " — SHE BEGAN FEEBLY.

shoes toeing out on the crack. It was over. She had
not failed before Squire Bean. For a few minutes,
she could think of nothing but that.

The rest of the class had their weak points, more-

over their strong points, overlooked in the presence
of the company. The first thing Patience knew, ever
so many had missed in the nine-table, and she had
gone up to the head.

Standing there, all at once a terrible misgiving
seized her. " I wouldn't have gone to the head if I
hadn't been told," she thought to herself. Martha
was next below her ; she knew that question in the
nines, her hand had been up, so had John Allen's and
Phœbe Adams'.

This was the last class before recess. Patience
went soberly out in the yard with the other girls. There
was a little restraint over all the scholars. They
looked with awe at the Squire's horse and chaise. The
horse was tied after a novel fashion, an invention of
the Squire's own. He had driven a gimlet into the
schoolhouse wall, and tied his horse to it with a stout
rope. Whenever the Squire drove he carried with
him his gimlet, in case there should be no hitching-
post. Occasionally house-owners rebelled, but it made
no difference ; the next time the Squire had occasion
to stop at their premises there was another gimlet-hole
in the wall. Few people could make their way good
against Squire Bean's.

There were a great many holes in the schoolhouse
walls, for the Squire made frequent visits ; he was one
of the committee and considered himself very necessary
for the well-being of the school. Indeed if he had

frankly spoken his mind, he would probably have admitted that in his estimation the school could not be
properly kept one day without his assistance.

Patience stood with her back against the school

" WHAT ! " SAID SQUIRE BEAN SUDDENLY.

fence, and watched the others soberly.   The girls
wanted her to play " Little Sally Waters sitting in the
sun," but she said no, she didn't want to play.

Martha took hold of her arm and tried to pull her
into the ring, but she held back.

" What is the matter ? " said Martha.

" Nothing," Patience said, but her face was full of
trouble. There was a little wrinkle between her re-
flective brown eyes, and she drew in her under lip after
a way she had when disturbed.

When the bell rang, the scholars filed in with the
greatest order and decorum. Even the most frisky
boys did no more than roll their eyes respectfully in
the Squire's direction as they passed him, and they
tiptoed on their bare feet in the most cautious manner.

The Squire sat through the remaining exercises, until
it was time to close the school.

" You may put up your books," said the teacher.
There was a rustle and clatter, then a solemn hush.
They all sat with their arms folded, looking expectantly
at Squire Bean. The teacher turned to him. Her
cheeks were very red, and she was very dignified, but
her voice shook a little.

" Won't you make some remarks to the pupils ? "
said she.

Then the Squire rose and cleared his throat. The
scholars did not pay much attention to what he said,
although they sat still, with their eyes riveted on his
face. But when, toward the close of his remarks, he
put his hand in his pocket, and a faint jingling was
heard, a thrill ran over the school.

The Squire pulled out two silver sixpences, and held them up impressively before the children. Through a hole in each of them dangled a palm-leaf strand; and the Squire's own initial was stamped on both.

"Thomas Arnold may step this way," said the Squire.

Thomas Arnold had acquitted himself well in geography, and to him the Squire duly presented one of the sixpences.

Thomas bobbed, and pattered back to his seat with all his mates staring and grinning at him.

Then Patience Mather's heart jumped — Squire Bean was bidding her step that way, on account of her going to the head of the arithmetic class. She sat still. There was a roaring in her ears. Squire Bean spoke again. Then the teacher interposed. "Patience," said she, "did you not hear what Squire Bean said? Step this way."

Then Patience rose and dragged slowly down the aisle. She hung her head, she dimly heard Squire Bean speaking; then the sixpence touched her hand. Suddenly Patience looked up. There was a vein of heroism in the little girl. Not far back, some of her kin had been brave fighters in the Revolution. Now their little descendant went marching up to her own enemy in her own way. She spoke right up before Squire Bean.

"I'd rather you'd give it to some one else," said she

with a curtesy. " It doesn't belong to me. I wouldn't have gone to the head if I hadn't cheated."

Patience's cheeks were white, but her eyes flashed. Squire Bean gasped, and turned it into a cough. Then he began asking her questions. Patience answered unflinchingly. She kept holding the sixpence toward him.

Finally he reached out and gave it a little push back.

" Keep it," said he ; " keep it, keep it. I don't give it to you for going to the head, but because you are an honest and truthful child."

Patience blushed pink to her little neck. She curtesied deeply and returned to her seat, the silver sixpence dangling from her agitated little hand. She put her head down on her desk, and cried, now it was all over, and did not look up till school was dismissed, and Martha Joy came and put her arm around her and comforted her.

The two little girls were very close friends, and were together all the time which they could snatch out of school hours. Not long after the presentation of the sixpence, one night after school, Patience's mother wanted her to go on an errand to Nancy Gookin's hut.

Nancy Gookin was an Indian woman, who did a good many odd jobs for the neighbors. Mrs. Mather was expecting company, and she wanted her to come the next day and assist her about some cleaning.

Patience was usually willing enough, but to-night she demurred.   In fact, she was a little afraid of the Indian woman, who lived all alone in a little hut on the edge of some woods.   Her mother knew it, but it was a foolish fear, and she did not encourage her in it.

"There is no sense in your being afraid of Nancy," she said with some severity.   "She's a good woman, if she is an Injun, and she is always to be seen in the meeting-house of a Sabbath day."

As her mother spoke, Patience could see Nancy's dark harsh old face peering over the pew, where she and some of her nation sat together, Sabbath days, and the image made her shudder in spite of its environments.   However, she finally put on her little sun-bonnet and set forth.   It was a lovely summer twilight; she had only about a quarter of a mile to go, but her courage failed her more and more at every step. Martha Joy lived on the way.   When she reached her house, she stopped and begged her to go with her. Martha was obliging; under ordinary circumstances she would have gone with alacrity, but to-night she had a hard toothache.   She came to the door with her face all tied up in a hop-poultice.   "I'm 'fraid I can't go," she said dolefully.

But Patience begged and begged.   "I'll spend my sixpence that uncle Joseph gave me, and I'll buy you a whole card of peppermints," said she finally, by way of inducement.

That won the day. Martha got few sweets, and if there was anything she craved, it was the peppermints, which came, in those days, in big beautiful cards, to be broken off at will. And to have a whole card!

So poor Martha tied her little flapping sunbonnet over her swollen cheeks, and went with Patience to see Nancy Gookin, who received the message thankfully, and did not do them the least harm in the world.

Martha had really a very hard toothache. She did not sleep much that night for all the hop-poultice, and she went to school the next day feeling tired and cross. She was a nervous little girl, and never bore illness very well. But to-day she had one pleasant anticipation. She thought often of that card of peppermints. It had cheered her somewhat in her uneasy night. She thought that Patience would surely bring them to school. She came early herself and watched for her. She entered quite late, just before the bell rang. Martha ran up to her. "I haven't got the peppermints," said Patience. She had been crying.

Martha straightened up: "Why not?"

The tears welled out of Patience's eyes. "I can't find that sixpence anywhere."

The tears came into Martha's eyes too. She looked as dignified as her poulticed face would allow. "I never knew you told fibs, Patience Mather," said she. "I don't believe my mother will want me to go with you any more."

Just then the bell rang. Martha went crying to her seat, and the others thought it was on account of her toothache. Patience kept back her tears. She was forming a desperate resolution. When recess came, she got permission to go to the store which was quite near, and she bought a card of peppermints with the Squire's sixpence. She had pulled out the palm-leaf strand on her way, thrusting it into her pocket guiltily. She felt as if she were committing sacrilege. These sixpences, which Squire Bean bestowed upon worthy scholars from time to time, were ostensibly for the purpose of book-marks. That was the reason for the palm-leaf strand. The Squire took the sixpences to the blacksmith who stamped them with B's, and then, with his own hands, he adjusted the palm-leaf.

The man who kept the store looked at the sixpence curiously, when Patience offered it.

" One of the Squire's sixpences ! " said he.

" Yes ; it's mine." That was the argument which Patience had set forth to her own conscience. It was certainly her own sixpence ; the Squire had given it to her — had she not a right to do as she chose with it ?

The man laughed ; his name was Ezra Tomkins, and he enjoyed a joke. He was privately resolving to give that sixpence in change to the old Squire and see what he would say. If Patience had guessed his thoughts —

But she took the card of peppermints, and carried them to the appeased and repentant and curious Martha, and waited further developments in trepidation. She had a presentiment deep within her childish soul that some day she would have a reckoning with Squire Bean concerning his sixpence.

If by chance she had to pass his house, she would hurry by at her utmost speed lest she be intercepted. She got out of his way as fast as she could if she spied his old horse and chaise in the distance. Still she knew the day would come ; and it did.

It was one Saturday afternoon; school did not keep, and she was all alone in the house with Martha. Her mother had gone visiting. The two little girls were playing " Holly Gull, Passed how many," with beans in the kitchen, when the door opened, and in walked Susan Elder. She was a woman who lived at Squire Bean's and helped his wife with the housework.

The minute Patience saw her, she knew what her errand was. She gave a great start. Then she looked at Susan Elder with her big frightened eyes.

Susan Elder was a stout old woman. She sat down on the settle, and wheezed before she spoke. " Squire Bean wants you to come up to his house right away," said she at last.

Patience trembled all over. " My mother is gone away. I don't know as she would want me to go," she ventured despairingly.

"He wants you to come right away," said Susan.

"I don't believe mother'd want me to leave the house alone."

"I'll stay an' rest till you git back; I'd jest as soon. I'm all tuckered out comin' up the hill."

Patience was very pale. She cast an agonized glance at Martha. "I spent the Squire's sixpence for those peppermints," she whispered. She had not told her before.

Martha looked at her in horror — then she begun to cry. "Oh! I made you do it," she sobbed.

"Won't you go with me?" groaned Patience.

"One little gal is enough," spoke up Susan Elder. "He won't like it if two goes."

That settled it. Poor little Patience Mather crept meekly out of the house and down the hill to Squire Bean's, without even Martha's foreboding sympathy for consolation.

She looked ahead wistfully all the way. If she could only see her mother coming — but she did not, and there was Squire Bean's house, square and white and massive, with great sprawling clumps of white peonies in the front yard.

She went around to the back door, and raised a feeble clatter with the knocker. Mrs. Squire Bean, who was tall and thin and mild-looking, answered her knock. "The — Squire — sent — for — me" — choked Patience.

"Oh!" said the old lady, "you air the little Mather-gal, I guess."

Patience shook so she could hardly reply.

"You'd better go right into his room," said Mrs. Squire Bean, and Patience followed her. She gave her a little pat when she opened a door on the right. "Don't you be afeard," said she; "he won't say nothin' to you. I'll give you a piece of sweet-cake when you come out."

Thus admonished, Patience entered. "Here's the little Mather-gal," Mrs. Bean remarked; then the door closed again on her mild old face.

When Patience first looked at that room, she had a wild impulse to turn and run. A conviction flashed through her mind that she could outrun Squire Bean and his wife easily. In fact, the queer aspect of the room was not calculated to dispel her nervous terror. Squire Bean's peculiarities showed forth in the arrangement of his room, as well as in other ways. His floor was painted drab, and in the center were the sun and solar system depicted in yellow. But that six-rayed yellow sun, the size of a large dinner plate, with its group of lesser six-rayed orbs as large as saucers, did not startle Patience as much as the rug beside the Squire's bed. That was made of a brindle cow-skin with — the horns on. The little girl's fascinated gaze rested on these bristling horns and could not tear itself away. Across the foot of the Squire's bed lay a great

LITTLE PATIENCE OBEYS THE SQUIRE'S SUMMONS.

iron bar; that was a housewifely scheme of his own to keep the clothes well down at the foot. But Patience's fertile imagination construed it into a dire weapon of punishment.

The Squire was sitting at his old cherry desk. He turned around and looked at Patience sharply from under his shaggy, overhanging brows.

Then he fumbled in his pocket and brought something out — it was the sixpence. Then he began talking. Patience could not have told what he said. Her mind was entirely full of what she had to say. Somehow she stammered out the story: how she had been afraid to go to Nancy Gookin's, and how she had lost the sixpence her uncle had given her, and how Martha had said she told a fib. Patience trembled and gasped out the words, and curtesied, once in a while, when the Squire said something.

"Come here," said he, when he had sat for a minute or two, taking in the facts of the case.

To Patience's utter astonishment, Squire Bean was laughing, and holding out the sixpence.

"Have you got the palm-leaf string?"

"Yes, sir," replied Patience, curtesying.

"Well, you may take this home, and put in the palm-leaf string, and use it for a marker in your book — but don't you spend it again."

"No, sir." Patience curtesied again.

"You did very wrong to spend it, very wrong.

Those sixpences are not given to you to spend. But I will overlook it this once."

The Squire extended the sixpence. Patience took it, with another dip of her little skirt. Then he turned around to his desk.

Patience waited a few minutes. She did not know whether she was dismissed or not. Finally the Squire begun to add aloud: "Five and five are ten," he said, "ought, and carry the one."

He was adding a bill. Then Patience stole out softly. Mrs. Squire Bean was waiting in the kitchen. She gave her a great piece of plum-cake and kissed her.

"He didn't hurt you any, did he?" said she.

"No, ma'am," said Patience, looking with a bewildered smile at the sixpence.

That night she tied in the palm-leaf strand again, and she put the sixpence in her Geography-book, and she kept it so safely all her life that her great-grandchildren have seen it.

A PLAIN CASE.

WILLY had his own little bag packed — indeed it had been packed for three whole days — and now he stood gripping it tightly in one hand, and a small yellow cane which was the pride of his heart in the other. Willy had a little harmless, childish dandyism about him which his mother rather encouraged. " I'd rather he'd be this way than the other," she said when people were inclined to smile at his little fussy habits. " It won't hurt him any to be nice and particular, if he doesn't get conceited."

Willy looked very dainty and sweet and gentle as he stood in the door this morning. His straight fair hair was brushed very smooth, his white straw hat with its blue ribbon was set on exactly, there was not a speck on his best blue suit.

"Willy looks as if he had just come out of the band-box," Grandma had said. But she did not have time to admire him long; she was not nearly ready herself. Grandma was always in a hurry at the last moment. Now she had to pack her big valise, brush Grandpa's hair, put on his " dicky " and cravat, and adjust her own bonnet and shawl.

Willy was privately afraid she would not be ready when the village coach came, and so they would miss the train, but he said nothing. He stood patiently in the door and looked down the street whence the coach would come, and listened to the bustle in Grandma's room. There was not an impatient line in his face although he had really a good deal at stake. He was going to Exeter with his Grandpa and Grandma, to visit his aunt Annie, and his new uncle Frank. Grandpa and Grandma had come from Maine to visit their daughter Ellen who was Willy's mother, and now they were going to see Annie. When Willy found out that he was going too, he was delighted. He had always been very fond of his aunt Annie, and had not seen her for a long time. He had never seen his new uncle Frank who had been married to Annie six months before, and he looked forward to that. Uncles and aunts seemed a very desirable acquisition to this little Willy, who had always been a great pet among his relatives.

" He won't make you a bit of trouble, if you don't mind taking him. He never teases nor frets, and he won't be homesick," his mother had told his grandmother.

" I know all about that," Grandma Stockton had replied. " I'd just as soon take him as a doll-baby."

Willy Norton really was a very sweet boy. He proved it this morning by standing there so patiently

WATCHING FOR THE COACH.

and never singing out, " Ain't you most ready, Grandma?" although it did seem to him she never would be.

His mother was helping her pack too; he could hear them talking. "I guess I sha'n't put in father's best coat," Grandma Stockton remarked, among other things. "He won't be in Exeter over Sunday, and won't want it to go to meetin', and it musses it up so to put it in a valise."

"Well, I don't know as I would as long as you're coming back here," said his mother.

After a while she remarked further, "If father should want that coat, you can send for it, and I can put in Willy's other shoes with it."

Willy noticed that, because he himself had rather regretted not taking his other shoes. He had only his best ones, and he thought he might want to go berrying in Exeter and would spoil them tramping through the bushes and briers, and he did not like to wear shabby shoes.

"Well, I can; but I guess he won't want it," said Grandma.

At last the coach came in sight, and Grandma was all ready excepting her bonnet and gloves, and Grandpa had only to brush his hat very carefully and put it on; so they did not miss the train.

Willy's mother hugged him tight and kissed him. There were tears in her eyes. This was the first time

he had ever been away from home without her.   " Be
a good boy," said she.

" There isn't any need of tellin' him that," chuckled
Grandpa, getting into the coach.   He thought Willy
was the most wonderful child in the world.

It was quite a long ride to Exeter.   They did not
get there until tea-time, but that made it seem all the
pleasanter.   Willy never forgot how peaceful and
beautiful that little, elm-shaded village looked with
the red light of the setting sun over it.   There was
aunt Annie, too, in the prettiest blue-sprigged, white
cambric, standing in her door watching for them; and
she was so surprised and delighted to see Willy, and
they had tea right away, and there were berries
and cream, and cream-tartar biscuits and frosted cake.

Uncle Frank, Willy thought, was going to be the
nicest uncle he had.   There was something about
the tall, curly-headed, pleasant-eyed young man which
won his boyish heart at once.

Glad to see you, sir," uncle Frank said in his
loud, merry voice; then he gave Willy's little slim
hand a big shake, as if it were a man's.

He was further prepossessed in his favor when, after
tea, he begged to take him over to the store and show
him around before he went to bed.   Grandma had
suggested his going directly to bed, as he must be
fatigued with the journey, but uncle Frank pleaded for
fifteen minutes' grace, so Willy went to view the store.

It was almost directly opposite uncle Frank's house, and uncle Frank and his father kept it. It was in a large old building, half of which was a dwelling-house where uncle Frank's parents lived, and where he had lived himself before he was married. The store was a large country one, and there was a post-office and an express office connected with it. Uncle Frank and his father were store-keepers and postmasters and express-agents.

The jolly new uncle gave Willy some sticks of peppermint and winter-green candy out of the glass jars, in the store-window, and showed him all around. He introduced him to his father, and took him into the house to see his mother. They made much of him, as strangers always did.

"They said I must call them Grandpa and Grandma Perry," he told his own grandmother when he got home.

He told her, furthermore, privately, when she came upstairs after he was in bed to see if everything was all right, that he thought Annie had shown very good taste in marrying uncle Frank. She told of it, downstairs, and there was a great laugh. "I don't know when I have taken such a fancy to a boy," uncle Frank said warmly. "He is so good, and yet he's smart enough, too."

"Everybody takes to him," his grandmother said proudly.

In a day or two Willy wrote a letter to his mother, and told her he was having the best time that he ever had in his life.

Willy was only seven years old and had never written many letters, but this was a very good one. His mother away down in Ashbury thought so. She shed a few tears over it. "It does seem as if I couldn't get along another day without seeing him," she told Willy's father; "but I'm glad if it is doing the dear child good, and he is enjoying it."

One reason why Willy had been taken upon the trip was his health. He had always been considered rather delicate. It did seem as if he had every chance to grow stronger in Exeter. The air was cool and bracing from the mountains; aunt Annie had the best things in the world to eat, and as he had said, he was really having a splendid time. He rode about with uncle Frank in the grocery wagon, he tended store, he fished, and went berrying. There were only two drawbacks to his perfect comfort. One came from his shoes. Grandpa Perry had found an old pair in the store, and he wore them on his fishing and berry-ing jaunts; but they were much too large and they slipped and hurt his heels. However he said nothing; he stumped along in them manfully, and tried to ignore such a minor grievance. Willy had really a stanch vein in him, in spite of his gentleness and mildness. The other drawback lay in the fact that the visit was to be of such short duration. It began Monday and was expected to end Saturday. Willy counted the hours; every night before he went to sleep he heaved a regretful sigh over the day which had just gone. It had been decided before leaving home that they were to return on Saturday, and he had had no intimation of any change of plan.

Friday morning he awoke with the thought, "this is the last day." However, Willy was a child, and, in the morning, a day still looked interminable to him, especially when there were good times looming up in it. To-day he expected to take a very long ride with uncle Frank, who was going to Keene to buy a new horse.

"I want Willy to go with me, to help pick him out," he told Grandma Stockton, and Willy took it in serious earnest. They were going to carry lunch and be gone all day. This promised pleasure looked so big to the boy, as he became wider awake, that he could see nothing at all beyond it, not even the sad departure and end of this delightful visit on the morrow. So he went down to breakfast as happy as ever.

"That boy certainly looks better," Grandpa Stockton remarked, as the coffee was being poured.

"We must have him weighed before he goes home," Grandma said, beaming at him.

"That's one thing I thought of, 'bout stayin' a week longer," Grandpa went on. "It seems to be doin'

Sonny, here, so much good." Grandpa had a very slow, deliberate way of speaking.

Willy laid down his spoon and stared at him, but he said nothing.

" I don't see what you were thinking of not to plan to stay longer in the first place," said aunt Annie. " I don't like it much." She made believe to pout her pretty lips.

" Well," said uncle Frank, " I'll send for that coat right away this morning, so you'll be sure to get it to-morrow night."

" Yes," said Grandpa, " I'd like to hev it to wear to meetin'.   Mother thinks my old one ain't just fit."

" No, it ain't," spoke up Grandma.   " It does well enough when you're at home, where folks know you, but it's different among strangers.   An' you've got to have it next week, anyhow."

Willy looked up at his grandmother.   "Grandma," said he tremblingly, " ain't we going home to-morrow ? "

" Why, bless the child ! " said she.   " I forgot he didn't know.   We talked about it last night after he'd gone to bed."

Then she explained.   They were going to stay another week.   Next week Wednesday, Grandpa and Grandma Perry had been married twenty-five years, and they were going to have a silver wedding.   So they were going to remain and be present at it, and Grandpa was going to send for his best coat to wear.

Willy looked so radiant that they all laughed, and uncle Frank said he was going to keep him always, and let him help him in the store.

Before they started off to buy the horse, uncle Frank telegraphed to Ashbury about the coat; he also mentioned Willy's shoes.

The two had a beautiful ride, and bought a handsome black horse. Uncle Frank consulted Willy a great deal about the purchase, and expatiated on his good judgment in the matter after they got home. One of Willy's chief charms was that he stood so much flattery of this kind, without being disagreeably elated by it. His frank, childish delight was always pretty to see.

The next afternoon he went berrying with a little boy who lived next door. At five o'clock aunt Annie ran over to the store to see if the coat had come.

" It has," she told her mother when she returned; " it came at one o'clock, and Mother Perry gave it to Willy to bring home."

" To Willy? Why, what did the child do with it?" Grandma said wonderingly. " He didn't bring it home."

" Maybe he carried it over to Josie Allen's and left it there." Josie Allen was the boy with whom Willy had gone berrying. His house stood very near uncle Frank's, and both were nearly across the road from the store.

" Well, maybe he did, he was in such a hurry to go berrying," said Grandma assentingly.

About six o'clock, when the family were all at the tea-table, Willy came clumping painfully in his big shoes into the yard. There were blisters on his small, delicate heels, but nobody knew it. His little fair face was red and tired, but radiant. His pail was heaped and rounded up with the most magnificent berries of the season.

"Just look here," said he, with his sweet voice all quivering with delight.

He stood outside on the piazza, and lifted the pail on to the window-sill. He could not wait until he came in to show these berries. He would have to walk way around through the kitchen in those irritating shoes.

They all exclaimed and admired them as much as he could wish, then Grandma said suddenly : " But what did you do with the coat, Willy ? "

" The coat ? " repeated Willy in a bewildered way.

" Yes; the coat. Did you take it over to Josie's an' leave it ? If you did, you must go right back and get it. Did you ? "

" No."

" Why, what did you do with it ? "

" I didn't do anything with it."

" William Dexter Norton ! what do you mean ? "

Everybody had stopped eating, and was staring out

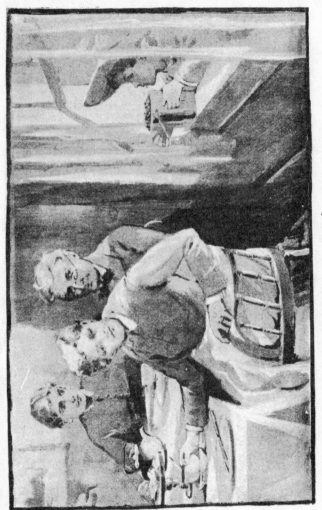

"JUST LOOK HERE!" SAID WILLY'S SWEET VOICE.

at Willy, who was staring in. His happy little red
face had suddenly turned sober.

"Come in, Sonny, an' we'll see what all the
trouble's about, an' straighten it out in a jiffy," spoke
up Grandpa. The contrast between Grandpa's slow
tones and the "jiffy" was very funny.

Willy crept slowly down the long piazza, through
the big kitchen into the dining-room.

"Now, Sonny, come right here," said his grandfather, "an' we'll have it all fixed up nice."

The boy kept looking from one face to another in a
wondering frightened way. He went hesitatingly up
to his grandfather, and stood still, his poor little
smarting feet toeing in, after a fashion they had, when
tired, the pail full of berries dangling heavily on his
slight arm.

"Now, Sonny, look up here, an' tell us all about it.
What did you do with Grandpa's coat, boy ? "

"I — didn't do anything with it."

"William," began his grandmother, but Grandpa
interrupted her. "Just wait a minute, mother," said
he. "Sonny an' I air goin' to settle this. Now,
Sonny, don't you get scared. You jest think a
minute. Think real hard, don't hurry — now, can't
you tell what you did with Grandpa's coat ? "

"I — didn't — do anything with it," said Willy.

"My sakes ! " said his grandmother. "What has
come to the child ? " She was very pale. Aunt

Annie and uncle Frank looked as it they did not know what to think. Grandpa himself settled back in his chair, and stared helplessly at Willy.

Finally aunt Annie tried her hand. "See here, Willy dear," said she, "you are tired and hungry and want your supper ; just tell us what you did with the coat after Grandma Perry gave it to you" —

"She didn't," said Willy.

That was dreadful. They all looked aghast at one another. Was Willy lying — Willy !

"Didn't — give — it — to you — Sonny !" said Grandpa, feebly, and more slowly than ever.

"No, sir."

Grandma Stockton had been called quick-tempered when she was a girl, and she gave proof of it some-times, even now in her gentle old age. She spoke very sternly and quickly: "Willy, we have had all of this nonsense that we want. Now you just speak right up an' tell the truth. What did you do with your grandfather's coat ? "

"I didn't do anything with it," faltered Willy again. His lip was quivering.

"What ? "

"I — didn't " — began the child again, then his sobs checked him. He crooked his little free arm, hid his face in the welcome curve, and cried in good earnest.

"Stop crying and tell me the truth," said Grandma pitilessly.

Willy again gasped out his one reply; he shook so that he could scarcely hold his berry pail. Aunt Annie took it out of his hand and set it on the table. Uncle Frank rose with a jerk. "I'll run over and get mother," said he, with an air that implied, "I'll soon settle this matter."

But the matter was very far from settled by Mrs. Perry's testimony. She only repeated what she had already told her daughter-in-law.

"The bundle came on the noon express," said she, "and I told Mr. Perry to set it down in the kitchen, and I would see that it got over to you. He didn't know how to stop just then. It laid there on one of the kitchen-chairs while I was clearing away the dinner-dishes. Then about two o'clock I was changing my dress, when I heard Willy whistling out in the yard, and I ran into the kitchen and got the bundle, and called him to take it. I opened the south door and gave it to him, and told him to take it right home to his grandpa. He said he guessed he'd open it and see if his shoes had come, and I told him 'no,' he must go straight home with it."

That was Mrs. Perry's testimony. Willy heard in the presence of all the family; then when the question as to the whereabouts of the coat was put to him, he made the same answer. He also repeated that Grandma Perry had not given it to him.

"Don't you let me hear you tell that wicked lie

again," said his Grandma Stockton. She was nearly as much agitated as the boy. She did not know what to do, and nobody else did.

Grandpa Perry came over with three sticks of twisted red and white peppermint candy, and three of barley. He caught hold of Willy and swung him on to his knee. He was a fleshy, jolly man.

"Now, sir," said he, "let's strike a bargain — I'll give you these six whole sticks of candy for your supper, and you tell me what you did with Grandpa's coat."

"I — didn't do — any " — Willy commenced between his painful sobs, but his grandmother interrupted — "Hush! don't you ever say that again," said she. "You did do something with it."

"I'll throw in a handful of raisins," said Mr. Perry. But it was of no use.

"Well, if the little chap was mine," said Mrs. Perry finally, "I should give him his supper and put him to bed, and see how he would look at it in the morning."

"I think that would be the best way," chimed in aunt Annie eagerly. "He's all tired out and hungry, and doesn't know what he does know — do you, dear?"

So she poured out some milk, and cut off a big slice of cake, but Willy did not want any supper. It was hard work to induce him to swallow a little milk before he went upstairs. His grandmother heaved a desperate sigh after he was gone.

" If it was in the days of the Salem witches," said
she, " I'd know just what to think; as 'tis, I don't."

" That boy was never known to tell a lie before in
his whole life — his mother said so. He never pestered
her the way some children do, lyin'; an' as for stealin'
— why, I'd trusted him with every cent I've got in
the world." That was Grandpa Stockton.

During the next two or three days every inducement
was brought to bear upon Willy. He was scolded and
coaxed, he was promised a reward if he would tell the
truth, he was assured that he should not be punished.
Monday he was kept in his room all day, and was
given nothing but bread and milk to eat. Severer
measures were hinted at, but Grandpa Stockton put
his foot down peremptorily. " That boy has never
been whipped in his whole life," said he, " an' his own
folks have got to begin it, if anybody does."

All the premises were searched for the missing coat,
but no trace of it was found. The mystery thickened
and deepened. How could a boy lose a coat going
across a road in broad daylight? Why would he not
confess that he had lost it?

Finally it was decided to take him home. He was
becoming all worn out with excitement and distress.
He was too delicate a child to long endure such a
strain. They thought that once at home his mother
might be able to do what none of the rest had.

All the others were getting worn out also. A good

many tears had been shed by the older members of the company. Poor Mrs. Perry took much blame to herself for giving the coat to the boy, and so opening the way for the difficulty.

"Mr. Perry says he thinks I ought not to have given the coat to him, he's nothing but a child, any way," she said tearfully once.

It was Monday afternoon when Willy was shut up in his room, and all the others were talking the matter over downstairs.

Tears stood in aunt Annie's blue eyes. "He's nothing but a baby," said she, "and if I had my way I'd call him downstairs and give him a cookie and never speak of the old coat again."

"You talk very silly, Annie," said Grandmother Stockton. "I hope you don't want to have the child to grow up a wicked, deceitful man."

Willy's grandparents gave up going to the silver wedding. Grandpa had no good coat to wear, and indeed neither of them had any heart to go.

So the morning of the wedding-day they started sadly to return to Ashbury. Willy's face looked thin and tear-stained. Somebody had packed his little bag for him, but he forgot his little cane.

When he was seated in the cars beside his grandmother, he began to cry. She looked at him a moment, then she put her arm around him, and drew his head down on her black cashmere shoulder.

" Tell Grandma, can't you," she whispered, " what you did with Grandpa's coat ? "

" I didn't — do — any " —

" Hush," said she, " don't you say that again, Willy ! " But she kept her arm around him.

Willy's mother came running to the door to meet them when they arrived. She had heard nothing of the trouble. She had only had a hurried message that they were coming to-day.

She threw her arms around Willy, then she held him back and looked at him. " Why, what is the matter with my precious boy ! " she cried.

" O, mamma, mamma, I didn't, I didn't do anything with it ! " he sobbed, and clung to her so frantically that she was alarmed.

" What does he mean, mother ? " she asked.

Her mother motioned her to be quiet. " Oh ! it isn't anything," said she. " You'd better give him his supper, and get him to bed ; he's all tired out. I'll tell you by and by," she motioned with her lips.

So Willy's mother soothed him all she could. " Of course you didn't, dear," said she. " Mamma knows you didn't. Don't you worry any more about it."

It was early, but she got some supper for him, and put him to bed, and sat beside him until he went to sleep. She told him over and over that she knew he " didn't," in reply to his piteous assertions, and all the time she had not the least idea what it was all about.

After he had fallen asleep she went downstairs, and Grandma Stockton told her.   Willy's father had come, and he also heard the story.

"There's some mistake about it," said he. "I'll make Willy tell me about it, to-morrow. Nothing is going to make me believe that he is persisting in a deliberate lie in this way."

Willy's mother was crying herself, now.   "He never — told me a lie in his whole dear little life," she sobbed, "and I don't believe he has now. Nothing will ever — make me believe so."

"Don't cry, Ellen," said her husband. "There's something about this that we don't understand."

It was all talked over and over that night, but they were no nearer understanding the case.

"I'll see what I can do with Willy in the morning," his father said again, when the discussion was ended for the night.

Willy was not awake at the breakfast hour next morning, so the family sat down without him. They were not half through the meal when there were some quick steps on the path outside; the door was jerked open, and there was aunt Annie and uncle Frank.

She had Willy's little yellow cane in her hand, and she looked as if she did not know whether to laugh or cry.

"It's found!" she cried out, "it's found! Oh! where is he?   He left his cane, poor little boy!"

Then she really sank into a chair and began to cry. There were exclamations and questions and finally they arrived at the solution of the mystery.

Poor little Willy had not done anything with Grandpa's coat. Mrs. Perry had not given it to him. She had — given it to another boy.

"Last night about seven o'clock," said uncle Frank, "Mr. Gilbert Hammond brought it into the store. It seems he sent his boy, who is just about Willy's age, and really looks some like him, for a bundle he expected to come by express. The boy was to have some shoes in it.

"I suppose mother caught a glimpse of him, and very likely she didn't have on her glasses, and can't see very well without them, and she thought he was Willy. She was changing her dress, too, and I dare say only opened the door a little way. Then the Hammond boy's got a grandfather, and the shoes and the whole thing hung together.

"Mr. Hammond said he meant to have brought the bundle back before, but they had company come the next day, and it was overlooked.

"Father and mother both came running over the minute they heard of it, and nothing would suit Annie but we should start right off on the night train, and come down here and explain. And, to tell the truth, I wanted to come myself — I felt as if we owed it to the poor little chappie."

Uncle Frank's own voice sounded husky. The thought of all the suffering that poor little innocent boy had borne was not a pleasant one.

Everything that could be done to atone to Willy was done. He was loved and praised and petted, as he had never been before; in a little while he seemed as well and happy as ever.

The next Christmas Grandpa Perry sent a beautiful little gold watch to him, and he was so delighted with it that his father said, "He doesn't worry a bit now about the trouble he had in Exeter. That watch doesn't seem to bring it to mind at all. How quickly children get over things. He has forgotten all about it."

But Willy Norton had not forgotten all about it. He was just as happy as ever. He had entirely forgiven Grandma Perry for her mistake. Next summer he was going to Exeter again and have a beautiful time; but a good many years would pass, and whenever he looked at that little gold watch, he would see double. It would have for him a background of his grandfather's best coat.

Innocence and truth can feel the shadow of unjust suspicion when others can no longer see it.

THE STRANGER IN THE VILLAGE.

"MARGARY," said her mother, "take the pitcher now, and fetch me some fresh, cool water from the well, and I will cook the porridge for supper."

"Yes, mother," said Margary. Then she put on her little white dimity hood, and got the pitcher, which was charmingly shaped, from the cupboard shelf. The cupboard was a three-cornered one beside the chimney. The cottage which Margary and her mother lived in, was very humble, to be sure, but it was very pretty. Vines grew all over it, and flowering bushes crowded close to the diamond-paned windows. There was a little garden at one side, with beds of pinks and violets in it, and a straw-covered beehive, and some raspberry bushes all yellow with fruit.

Inside the cottage, the floor was sanded with the whitest sand; lovely old straight-backed chairs stood about; there was an oaken table, and a spinning-wheel. A wicker cage, with a lark in it, hung in the window.

Margary with her pitcher, tripped along to the village well. On the way she met two of her little mates — Rosamond and Barbara. They were flying along, their cheeks very rosy and their eyes shining.

"O, Margary," they cried, "come up to the tavern, quick, and see! The most beautiful coach-and-four is drawn up there. There are lackeys in green and gold, with cocked hats, and the coach hath a crest on the side — O, Margary!"

Margary's eyes grew large too, and she turned about with her empty pitcher and followed her friends. They had almost reached the tavern, and were in full sight of the coach-and-four, when some one coming toward them caused them to draw up on one side of the way and stare with new wonder. It was a most beautiful little boy. His golden curls hung to his shoulders, his sweet face had an expression at once gentle and noble, and his dress was of the richest material. He led a little flossy white dog by a ribbon.

After he had passed by, the three little girls looked at each other.

"Oh!" cried Rosamond, "did you see his hat and feather?"

"And his lace vandyke, and the fluffy white dog!" cried Barbara. But Margary said nothing. In her heart, she thought she had never seen any one so lovely.

Then she went on to the well with her pitcher, and Rosamond and Barbara went home, telling every one they met about the beautiful little stranger.

Margary, after she had filled her pitcher, went home also; and was beginning to talk about the stranger to

THE LITTLE STRANGER.

her mother, when a shadow fell across the floor from the doorway. Margary looked up. "There he is now!" cried she in a joyful whisper.

The pretty boy stood there indeed, looking in modestly and wishfully. Margary's mother arose at once from her spinning-wheel, and came forward; she was a very courteous woman. "Wilt thou enter, and rest thyself," said she, "and have a cup of our porridge, and a slice of our wheaten bread, and a bit of honeycomb?"

The little boy sniffed hungrily at the porridge which was just beginning to boil; he hesitated a moment, but finally thanked the good woman very softly and sweetly and entered.

Then Margary and her mother set a bottle of cowslip wine on the table, slices of wheaten bread, and a plate of honeycomb, a bowl of ripe raspberries, and a little jug of yellow cream, and another little bowl with a garland of roses around the rim, for the porridge. Just as soon as that was cooked, the stranger sat down, and ate a supper fit for a prince. Margary and her mother half supposed he was one; he had such a courtly, yet modest air.

When he had eaten his fill, and his little dog had been fed too, he offered his entertainers some gold out of a little silk purse, but they would not take it.

So he took hold of his dog's ribbon, and went away with many thanks. "We shall never see him again," said Margary sorrowfully.

" The memory of a stranger one has fed, is a pleasant one," said her mother.

" I am glad the lark sang so beautifully all the while he was eating," said Margary.

While they were eating their own supper, the oldest woman in the village came in. She was one hundred and twenty years old, and, by reason of her great age, was considered very wise.

" Have you seen the stranger?" asked she in her piping voice, seating herself stiffly.

" Yes," replied Margary's mother. " He hath supped with us."

The oldest woman twinkled her eyes behind her iron-bowed spectacles. " Lawks!" said she. But she did not wish to appear surprised, so she went on to say she had met him on the way, and knew who he was.

" He's a Lindsay," said the oldest woman, with a nod of her white-capped head. " I tried him wi' a buttercup. I held it under his chin, and he loves butter. So he's a Lindsay; all the Lindsays love butter. I know, for I was nurse in the family a hundred years ago."

This, of course, was conclusive evidence. Margary and her mother had faith in the oldest woman's opinion; and so did all the other villagers. She told a good many people how the little stranger was a Lindsay, before she went to bed that night. And he really was a Lindsay, too; though it was singular how the oldest woman divined it with a buttercup.

The pretty child had straightway driven off in his coach-and-four as soon as he had left Margary's mother's cottage; he had only stopped to have some defect in the wheels remedied. But there had been time enough for a great excitement to be stirred up in the village.

All any one talked about the next day, was the stranger. Every one who had seen him, had some new and more marvelous item; till charming as the child really was, he became, in the popular estimation, a real fairy prince.

When Margary and the other children went to school, with their horn-books hanging at their sides, they found the schoolmaster greatly excited over it. He was a verse-maker, and though he had not seen the stranger himself, his imagination more than made amends for that. So the scholars were not under a very strict rule that day, for the master was busy composing a poem about the stranger. Every now and then a line of the poem got mixed in with the lessons.

The schoolmaster told in beautiful meters about the stranger's rich attire, and his flowing locks of real gold wire, his lips like rubies, and his eyes like diamonds. He furnished the little dog with hair of real floss silk, and called his ribbon a silver chain. Then the coach, as it rolled along, presented such a dazzling appearance, that several persons who inadvertently looked at it had been blinded. It was the schoolmaster's opinion, set forth in his poem, that this really was a prince. One could scarcely doubt it, on reading the poem. It is a pity it has not been preserved, but it was destroyed — how, will transpire further on.

Well, two days after this dainty stranger with his coach-and-four came to the village, a little wretched beggar-boy, leading by a dirty string a forlorn muddy little dog, appeared on the street. He went to the tavern first, but the host pushed him out of the door, throwing a pewter porringer after him, which hit the poor little dog and made it yelp. Then he spoke pitifully to the people he met, and knocked at the cottage doors; but every one drove him away. He met the oldest woman, but she gathered her skirts closely around her and hobbled by, her pointed nose up in the air, and her cap-strings flying straight out behind.

" I prithee, granny," he called after her, " try me with the buttercup again, and see if I be not a Lindsay."

" Thou a Lindsay," quoth the oldest woman contemptuously ; but she was very curious, so she turned around and held a buttercup underneath the boy's dirty chin.

" Bah," said the oldest woman, " a Lindsay indeed ! Butter hath no charm for thee, and the Lindsays all loved it. I know, for I was nurse in the family a hundred year ago."

Then she hobbled away faster than ever, and the poor boy kept on. Then he met the schoolmaster, who had his new poem in a great roll in his hand. "What little vagabond is this?" muttered he, gazing at him with disgust. "He hath driven a fine metaphor out of my head."

When the boy reached the cottage where Margary and her mother lived, the dame was sitting in the door spinning, and the little girl was picking roses from a bush under the window, to fill a tall china mug which they kept on a shelf.

When Margary heard the gate click, and turning, saw the boy, she started so that she let her pinafore full of roses slip, and the flowers all fell out on the ground. Then she dropped an humble curtesy; and her mother rose and curtesied also, though she had not recognized her guest as soon as Margary.

The poor little stranger fairly wept for joy. "Ah, you remember me," he said betwixt smiles and tears.

Then he entered the cottage, and while Margary and her mother got some refreshment ready for him, he told his pitiful story.

His father was a Lindsay, and a very rich and noble gentleman. Some little time before, he and his little son had journeyed to London, with their coach-and-four. Business having detained him longer than he had anticipated, and fearing his lady might be uneasy, he had sent his son home in advance, in the coach, with his lackeys and attendants. Everything had gone safely till after leaving this village. Some miles beyond, they had been attacked by highwaymen and robbed. The servants had either been taken prisoners or fled. The thieves had driven off with the coach-and-four, and the poor little boy had crawled back to the village.

Margary and her mother did all they could to comfort him. They prepared some hot broth for him, and opened a bottle of cowslip wine. Margary's mother gave him some clean clothes, which had belonged to her son who had died. The little gentleman looked funny in the little rustic's blue smock, but he was very comfortable. They fed the forlorn little dog too, and washed him till his white hair looked fluffy and silky again.

When the London mail stopped in the village, the next day, they sent a message to Lord Lindsay, and in a week's time, he came after his son. He was a very grand gentleman; his dress was all velvet and satin, and blazing with jewels. How the villagers stared. They had flatly refused to believe that this last little stranger was the first one, and had made great fun of Margary and her mother for being so credulous. But they had not minded. They had given their guest a little pallet stuffed with down, and a pillow stuffed with rose-leaves to sleep on, and fed him with the best they had. His father, in his gratitude, offered Margary's mother rich rewards ; but she would take nothing. The little boy cried on parting with his kind friends, and Margary cried too.

" I prithee, pretty Margary, do not forget me," said he.

And she promised she never would, and gave him a sprig of rosemary out of her garden to wear for a breastknot.

The villagers were greatly mortified when they discovered the mistake they had made. However, the oldest woman always maintained that her not having her spectacles on, when she met the stranger the second time, was the reason of her not seeing that he loved butter ; and the schoolmaster gave his poetical abstraction for an excuse. Mine host of the " Boar's Head " fairly tore his hair, and flung the pewter porringer, which he had thrown after the stranger and his dog, into the well. After that he was very careful how he turned away strangers because of their appearance. Generally he sent for the oldest woman to put her spectacles on, and try the buttercup test. Then, if she said they loved butter and were Lindsays, they were taken in and entertained royally. She generally did say they loved butter — she was so afraid of making a mistake the second time, herself ; so the village-inn got to be a regular refuge for beggars, and they called it amongst themselves the " Beggars' Rest," instead of the " Boar's Head."

As for Margary, she grew up to be the pride of the village ; and in time, Lord Lindsay's son, who had always kept the sprig of rosemary, came and married her. They had a beautiful wedding ; all of the villagers were invited ; the bridegroom did not cherish any resentment. They danced on the green, and the Lindsay pipers played for them. The bride wore a white damask petticoat worked with pink roses, her pink satin shortgown was looped up with garlands of them, and she wore a wreath of roses on her head.

The oldest woman came to the wedding, and hobbled up to the bridegroom with a buttercup. "Thou beest a Lindsay," said she. "Thou lovest butter, and the Lindsays all did. I know, for I was nurse in the family a hundred year ago."

As for the schoolmaster, he was distressed. His wife had taken his poém on the stranger for papers to curl her hair on for the wedding, and he had just discovered it. He had calculated on making a present of it to the young couple.

However, he wrote another on the wedding, of which one verse is still extant, and we will give it :

> " When Lindsay wedded Margary,
> Merrily piped the pipers all.
> The bride, the village-pride was she,
> The groom, a gay gallant was he.
> Merrily piped the pipers all,
> When Lindsay wedded Margary."

THE BOUND GIRL.

THIS Indenture Wittnesseth, That I Margaret Burjust of Boston, in the County of Suffolk and Province of the Massachusetts Bay in New England. Have placed, and by these presents do place and bind out my only Daughter whose name is Ann Ginnins to be an Apprentice unto Samuel Wales and his wife of Braintree in the County afores: ᵈ, Blacksmith. To them and their Heirs and with them the s: ᵈ Samuel Wales, his wife and their Heirs, after the manner of an apprentice to dwell and Serve from the day of the date hereof for and during the full and Just Term of Sixteen years, three months and twenty-three day's next ensueing and fully to be Compleat, during all which term the s: ᵈ apprentice her s: ᵈ Master and Mistress faithfully Shall Serve, Their Secrets keep close, and Lawful and reasonable Command everywhere gladly do and perform.

Damage to her s: ᵈ Master and Mistress she shall not willingly do. Her s: ᵈ Master's goods she shall not waste, Embezel, purloin or lend unto Others nor suffer the same to be wasted or purloined. But to her power Shall discover the Same to her s: ᵈ Master. Taverns or Ailhouss she Shall not frequent, at any unlawful game She Shall not play, Matrimony she Shall not Contract with any persons during s: ᵈ Term. From her master's Service She Shall not at any time unlawfully absent herself. But in all things as a good honest and faithful Servant and apprentice Shall bear and behave herself, During the full term afores: ᵈ Commencing from the third day of November Anno Dom: One Thousand, Seven Hundred fifty and three. And the s: ᵈ Master for himself, wife, and Heir's, Doth Covenant Promise Grant and Agree unto and with the s: ᵈ apprentice and the s: ᵈ Margaret Burjust, in manner and form following. That is to say, That

273

they will teach the s : ᵈ apprentice or Cause her to be taught in
the Art of good housewifery, and also to read and write well.
And will find and provide for and give unto s : ᵈ apprentice good
and sufficient Meat Drink washing and lodging both in Sickness
and in health, and at the Expiration of s : ᵈ term to Dismiss s : ᵈ
apprentice with two Good Suits of Apparrel both of woolen and
linnin for all parts of her body (viz) One for Lord-days and one
for working days Suitable to her Quality. In Testimony whereof
I Samuel Wales and Margaret Burjust Have Interchangably
Sett their hands and Seals this Third day November Anno Dom :
1753, and in the twenty-Seventh year of the Reign of our Sove-
raig'n Lord George the Second of great Britain the King.
    Signed Sealed & Delivered.
        In presence of
        SAM VAUGHAN   MARGARET BURGIS
        MARY VAUGHAN   her X mark.

This quaint document was carefully locked up, with
some old deeds and other valuable papers, in his desk,
by the "s : ᵈ Samuel Wales," one hundred and thirty
years ago.   The desk was a rude, unpainted pine affair,
and it reared itself on its four stilt-like legs in a corner
of his kitchen, in his house in the South Precinct of
Braintree.   The sharp eyes of the little "s : ᵈ apprentice " had noted it oftener and more enviously than any
other article of furniture in the house.   On the night
of her arrival, after her journey of fourteen miles from
Boston, over a rough bridle-road, on a jolting horse,
clinging tremblingly to her new " Master," she peered
through her little red fingers at the desk swallowing up
those precious papers which Samuel Wales drew from
his pocket with an important air.   She was hardly five

years old, but she was an acute child; and she watched her master draw forth the papers, show them to his wife, Polly, and lock them up in the desk, with the full understanding that they had something to do with her coming to this strange place; and, already, a shadowy purpose began to form itself in her mind.

She sat on a cunning little wooden stool, close to the fireplace, and kept her small chapped hands persistently over her face; she was scared, and grieved, and, withal, a trifle sulky. Mrs. Polly Wales cooked some Indian meal mush for supper in an iron pot swinging from its trammel over the blazing logs, and cast scrutinizing glances at the little stranger. She had welcomed her kindly, taken off her outer garments, and established her on the little stool in the warmest corner, but the child had given a very ungracious response. She would not answer a word to Mrs. Wales' coaxing questions, but twitched herself away with all her small might, and kept her hands tightly over her eyes, only peering between her fingers when she thought no one was noticing.

She had behaved after the same fashion all the way from Boston, as Mr. Wales told his wife in a whisper. The two were a little dismayed at the whole appearance of the small apprentice; to tell the truth, she was not in the least what they had expected. They had been revolving this scheme of taking "a bound girl" for some time in their minds; and Samuel Wales' gossip in Boston, Sam Vaughan, had been requested to keep a lookout for a suitable person.

So, when word came that one had been found, Mr. Wales had started at once for the city. When he saw the child, he was dismayed. He had expected to see a girl of ten; this one was hardly five, and she had anything but the demure and decorous air which his Puritan mind esteemed becoming and appropriate in a little maiden. Her hair was black and curled tightly, instead of being brown and straight parted in the middle, and combed smoothly over her ears as his taste regulated ; her eyes were black and flashing, instead of being blue, and downcast. The minute he saw the child, he felt a disapproval of her rise in his heart, and also something akin to terror. He dreaded to take this odd-looking child home to his wife Polly ; he foresaw contention and mischief in their quiet household. But he felt as if his word was rather pledged to his gossip, and there was the mother, waiting and expectant. She was a red-cheeked English girl, who had been in Sam Vaughan's employ ; she had recently married one Burjust, and he was unwilling to support the first husband's child, so this chance to bind her out and secure a good home for her had been eagerly caught at.

The small Ann seemed rather at Samuel Wales' mercy, and he had not the courage to disappoint his friend or her mother ; so the necessary papers were made out, Sam Vaughan's and wife's signatures affixed, and Margaret Burjust's mark, and he set out on his homeward journey with the child.

The mother was coarse and illiterate, but she had some natural affection; she "took on" sadly when the little girl was about to leave her, and Ann clung to her frantically. It was a pitiful scene, and Samuel Wales, who was a very tender-hearted man, was glad when it was over, and he jogging along the bridle-path.

But he had had other troubles to encounter. All at once, as he rode through Boston streets, with his little charge behind him, after leaving his friend's house, he felt a vicious little twitch at his hair, which he wore in a queue tied with a black ribbon after the fashion of the period. Twitch, twitch, twitch! The water came into Samuel Wales' eyes, and the blood to his cheeks, while the passers-by began to hoot and laugh. His horse became alarmed at the hubbub, and started up. For a few minutes the poor man could do nothing to free himself. It was wonderful what strength the little creature had; she clinched her tiny fingers in the braid, and pulled, and pulled. Then, all at once, her grasp slackened, and off flew her master's steeple-crowned hat into the dust, and the neat black ribbon on the end of the queue followed it. Samuel Wales reined up his horse with a jerk then, and turned round, and administered a sounding box on each of his apprentice's ears. Then he dismounted, amid shouts of laughter from the spectators, and got a man to hold the horse while he went back and picked up his hat and ribbon.

He had no further trouble. The boxes seemed to have subdued Ann effectually. But he pondered uneasily all the way home on the small vessel of wrath which was perched up behind him, and there was a tingling sensation at the roots of his queue. He wondered what Polly would say. The first glance at her face, when he lifted Ann off the horse at his own door, confirmed his fears. She expressed her mind, in a womanly way, by whispering in his ear at the first opportunity, " She's as black as an Injun."

After Ann had eaten her supper, and had been tucked away between some tow sheets and homespun blankets in a trundle-bed, she heard the whole story, and lifted up her hands with horror. Then the good couple read a chapter, and prayed, solemnly vowing to do their duty by this child which they had taken under their roof, and imploring Divine assistance.

As time wore on, it became evident that they stood in sore need of it. They had never had any children of their own, and Ann Ginnins was the first child who had ever lived with them. But she seemed to have the freaks of a dozen or more in herself, and they bade fair to have the experience of bringing up a whole troop with this one. They tried faithfully to do their duty by her, but they were not used to children, and she was a very hard child to manage. A whole legion of mischievous spirits seemed to dwell in her at times, and she became in a small and comparatively innocent way, the scandal of the staid Puritan neighborhood in which she lived. Yet, withal, she was so affectionate, and seemed to be actuated by so little real malice in any of her pranks, that people could not help having a sort of liking for the child, in spite of them.

She was quick to learn, and smart to work, too, when she chose. Sometimes she flew about with such alacrity that it seemed as if her little limbs were hung on wires, and no little girl in the neighborhood could do her daily tasks in the time she could, and they were no inconsiderable tasks, either.

Very soon after her arrival she was set to " winding quills," so many every day. Seated at Mrs. Polly's side, in her little homespun gown, winding quills through sunny forenoons — how she hated it. She liked feeding the hens and pigs better, and when she got promoted to driving the cows, a couple of years later, she was in her element. There were charming possibilities of nuts and checkerberries and sassafras and sweet flag all the way between the house and the pasture, and the chance to loiter, and have a romp.

She rarely showed any unwillingness to go for the cows; but once, when there was a quilting at her mis-

tress's house, she demurred.   It was right in the midst
of the festivities ; they were just preparing for supper,
in fact.   Ann knew all about the good things in the
pantry, she was wild with delight at the unwonted stir,
and anxious not to lose a minute of it.   She thought
some one else might go for the cows that night.   She
cried and sulked, but there was no help for it.   Go
she had to.   So she tucked up her gown — it was her
best Sunday one — took her stick, and trudged along.
When she came to the pasture, there were her master's
cows waiting at the bars.   So were Neighbor Belcher's
cows also, in the adjoining pasture.   Ann had her
hand on the topmost of her own bars, when she happened to glance over at Neighbor Belcher's, and a
thought struck her.   She burst into a peal of laughter,
and took a step towards the other bars.   Then she
went back to her own.   Finally, she let down the
Belcher bars, and the Belcher cows crowded out, to the
great astonishment of the Wales cows, who stared over
their high rails and mooed uneasily.

Ann drove the Belcher cows home and ushered them
into Samuel Wales' barnyard with speed.   Then she
went demurely into the house.   The table looked beautiful.   Ann was beginning to quake inwardly, though
she still was hugging herself, so to speak, in secret
enjoyment of her own mischief.   She had one hope —
that supper would be eaten before her master milked.
But the hope was vain.   When she saw Mr. Wales

come in, glance her way, and then call his wife out, she knew at once what had happened, and begun to tremble — she knew perfectly what Mr. Wales was saying out there. It was this: "That little limb has driven home all Neighbor Belcher's cows instead of ours; what's going to be done with her?"

She knew what the answer would be, too. Mrs. Polly was a peremptory woman.

Back Ann had to go with the Belcher cows, fasten them safely in their pasture again, and drive her master's home. She was hustled off to bed, then, without any of that beautiful supper. But she had just crept into her bed in the small unfinished room upstairs where she slept, and was lying there sobbing, when she heard a slow, fumbling step on the stairs. Then the door opened, and Mrs. Deacon Thomas Wales, Samuel Wales' mother, came in. She was a good old lady, and had always taken a great fancy to her son's bound girl; and Ann, on her part, minded her better than any one else. She hid her face in the tow sheet, when she saw grandma. The old lady had on a long black silk apron. She held something concealed under it, when she came in. Presently she displayed it.

"There — child," said she, " here's a piece of sweet cake and a couple of simballs, that I managed to save out for you. Jest set right up and eat 'em, and don't ever be so dretful naughty again, or I don't know what will become of you."

This reproof, tempered with sweetness, had a salutary effect on Ann. She sat up, and ate her sweet cake and simballs, and sobbed out her contrition to grandma, and there was a marked improvement in her conduct for some days.

Mrs. Polly was a born driver. She worked hard herself, and she expected everybody about her to. The tasks which Ann had set her did not seem as much out of proportion, then, as they would now. Still, her mistress, even then, allowed her less time for play than was usual, though it was all done in good faith, and not from any intentional severity. As time went on, she grew really quite fond of the child, and she was honestly desirous of doing her whole duty by her. If she had had a daughter of her own, it is doubtful if her treatment of her would have been much different.

Still, Ann was too young to understand all this, and, sometimes, though she was strong and healthy, and not naturally averse to work, she would rebel when her mistress set her stints so long, and kept her at work when other children were playing.

Once in a while she would confide in grandma, when Mrs. Polly sent her over there on an errand and she had felt unusually aggrieved because she had had to wind quills, or hetchel, instead of going berrying, or some like pleasant amusement.

"Poor little cosset," grandma would say, pityingly.

Then she would give her a simball, and tell her she must " be a good girl, and not mind if she couldn't play jest like the others, for she'd got to airn her own livin', when she grew up, and she must learn to work."

Ann would go away comforted, but grandma would be privately indignant. She was, as is apt to be the case, rather critical with her sons' wives, and she thought " Sam'l's kept that poor little gal too stiddy at work," and wished and wished she could shelter her under her own grandmotherly wing, and feed her with simballs to her heart's content. She was too wise to say anything to influence the child against her mistress, however. She was always cautious about that, even while pitying her. Once in a while she would speak her mind to her son, but he was easy enough — Ann would not have found him a hard task-master.

Still, Ann did not have to work hard enough to hurt her. The worst consequences were that such a rigid rein on such a frisky little colt perhaps had more to do with her " cutting up," as her mistress phrased it, than she dreamed of. Moreover the thought of the indentures, securely locked up in Mr. Wales' tall wooden desk, was forever in Ann's mind. Half by dint of questioning various people, half by her own natural logic she had settled it within herself, that at any time the possession of these papers would set her free, and she could go back to her own mother, whom she dimly remembered as being loud-voiced, but merry,

and very indulgent.   However, Ann·never meditated
in earnest, taking the indentures; indeed, the desk
was always locked — it held other documents more
valuable than hers — and Samuel Wales carried the
key in his waistcoat-pocket.

She went to a dame's school three months every
year. Samuel Wales carted half a cord of wood to
pay for her schooling, and she learned to write and
read in the New England Primer. Next to her, on
the split log bench, sat a little girl named Hannah
French. The two became fast friends. Hannah was
an only child, pretty and delicate, and very much
petted by her parents. No long hard tasks were set
those soft little fingers, even in those old days when
children worked as well as their elders. Ann admired
and loved Hannah, because she had what she, herself,
had not ; and Hannah loved and pitied Ann because
she had not what she had. It was a sweet little friend-
ship, and would not have been, if Ann had not been
free from envy and Hannah humble and pitying.

When Ann told her what a long stint she had to
do before school, Hannah would shed sympathizing
tears.

Ann, after a solemn promise of secrecy, told her
about the indentures one day. Hannah listened with
round, serious eyes; her brown hair was combed
smoothly down over her ears. She was a veritable
little Puritan damsel herself.

"If I could only get the papers, I wouldn't have to mind her, and work so hard," said Ann.

Hannah's eyes grew rounder. "Why, it would be sinful to take them!" said she.

Ann's cheeks blazed under her wondering gaze, and she said no more.

When she was about eleven years old, one icy January day, Hannah wanted her to go out and play on the ice after school. They had no skates, but it was rare fun to slide. Ann went home and asked Mrs. Polly's permission with a beating heart; she promised to do a double stint next day, if she would let her go. But her mistress was inexorable — work before play, she said, always; and Ann must not forget that she was to be brought up to work; it was different with her from what it was with Hannah French. Even this she meant kindly enough, but Ann saw Hannah go away. and sat down to her spinning with more fierce defiance in her heart than had ever been there before. She had been unusually good, too, lately. She always was, during the three months' schooling, with sober, gentle little Hannah French.

She had been spinning sulkily a while, and it was almost dark, when a messenger came for her master and mistress to go to Deacon Thomas Wales', who had been suddenly taken very ill.

Ann would have felt sorry if she had not been so angry. Deacon Wales was almost as much of a favorite of hers as his wife.   As it was, the principal thing she thought of, after Mr. Wales and his wife had gone, was that the key was in the desk.   However it had happened, there it was.   She hesitated a moment.   She was all alone in the kitchen, and her heart was in a tumult of anger, but she had learned her lessons from the Bible and the New England Primer, and she was afraid of the sin.   But at last she opened the desk, found the indentures, and hid them in the little pocket which she wore tied about her waist, under her petticoat.

Then Ann threw her blanket over her head, and got her poppet out of the chest.   The poppet was a little doll manufactured from a corn-cob, dressed in an indigo-colored gown.   Grandma had made it for her, and it was her chief treasure.   She clasped it tight to her bosom, and ran across lots to Hannah French's.

Hannah saw her coming, and met her at the door.

" I've brought you my poppet," whispered Ann, all breathless, "and you must keep her always, and not let her work too hard.   I'm going away ! "

Hannah's eyes looked like two solemn moons. " Where are you going, Ann ? "

" I'm going to Boston to find my own mother." She said nothing about the indentures to Hannah — somehow she could not.

Hannah could not say much, she was so astonished,

but as soon as Ann had gone, scudding across the fields, she went in with the poppet and told her mother.

Deacon Thomas Wales was very sick. Mr. and Mrs. Samuel remained at his house all night, but Ann was not left alone, for Mr. Wales had an apprentice who slept in the house.

Ann did not sleep any that night. She got up very early, before any one was stirring, and dressed herself in her Sunday clothes. Then she tied up her working clothes in a bundle, crept softly downstairs, and out doors.

It was bright moonlight and quite cold. She ran along as fast as she could on the Boston road. Deacon Thomas Wales's house was on the way. The windows were lit up. She thought of grandma and poor grandpa, with a sob in her heart, but she sped along. Past the schoolhouse, and meeting-house, too, she had to go, with big qualms of grief and remorse. But she kept on. She was a fast traveler.

She had reached the North Precinct of Braintree by daylight. So far, she had not encountered a single person. Now she heard horse's hoofs behind her. She began to run faster, but it was of no use. Soon Captain Abraham French loomed up on his big gray horse, a few paces from her. He was Hannah's father, but he was a tithing-man, and looked quite stern, and Ann had always stood in great fear of him.

She ran on as fast as her little heels could fly, with

a thumping heart. But it was not long before she felt herself seized by a strong arm and swung up behind Captain French on the gray horse. She was in a panic of terror, and would have cried and begged for mercy if she had not been in so much awe of her captor. She thought with awful apprehension of these stolen indentures in her little pocket. What if he should find that out!

Captain French whipped up his horse, however, and hastened along without saying a word. His silence, if anything, caused more dread in Ann than words would have. But his mind was occupied. Deacon Thomas Wales was dead ; he was one of his most beloved and honored friends, and it was a great shock to him. Hannah had told him about Ann's premeditated escape, and he had set out on her track as soon as he had found that she was really gone, that morning. But the news which he had heard on his way, had driven all thoughts of reprimand which he might have entertained, out of his head. He only cared to get the child safely back.

So not a word spoke Captain French, but rode on in grim and sorrowful silence, with Ann clinging to him, till he reached her master's door. Then he set her down with a stern and solemn injunction never to transgress again, and rode away.

Ann went into the kitchen with a quaking heart. It was empty and still. Its very emptiness and still-

ness seemed to reproach her. There stood the desk —
she ran across to it, pulled the indentures from her
pocket, put them in their old place, and shut the lid
down. There they staid till the full and just time of
her servitude had expired. She never disturbed them
again.

On account of the grief and confusion incident on
Deacon Wales's death, she escaped with very little cen-
sure. She never made an attempt to run away again.
Indeed, she had no wish to, for after Deacon Wales's
death, grandma was lonely and wanted her, and she
lived most of the time with her. And, whether she
was in reality treated any more kindly or not, she was
certainly happier.

DEACON THOMAS WALES'S WILL.

In the Name of God Amen! the Thirteenth Day of September One Thousand Seven Hundred Fifty & eight, I, Thomas Wales of Braintree, in the County of Suffolk & Province of the Massachusetts Bay in New England, Gent -- being in good health of Body and of Sound Disproving mind and Memory, Thanks be given to God — Calling to mind my mortality, Do therefore in my health make and ordain this my Last Will and Testament. And First I Recommend my Soul into the hand of God who gave it — Hoping through grace to obtain Salvation thro' the merits and Mediation of Jesus Christ my only Lord and Dear Redeemer, and my body to be Decently inter^d, at the Discretion of my Executor, believing at the General Resurection to receive the Same again by the mighty Power of God — And such worldly estate as God in his goodness hath graciously given me after Debts, funeral Expenses &c, are Paid I give & Dispose of the Same as Followeth —

Imprimis — I Give to my beloved Wife Sarah a good Sute of mourning apparrel Such as she may Choose — also if she acquit my estate of Dower and third-therin (as we have agreed) Then that my Executor return all of Household movables she bought at our marriage & since that are remaining, also to Pay to her or Her Heirs That Note of Forty Pound I gave to her, when she acquited my estate and I hers. Before Division to be made as herein exprest, also the Southwest fire-Room in my House, a right in my Cellar, Halfe the Garden, also the Privilege of water at the well & yard room and to bake in the oven what she hath need of to improve her Life-time by her.

After this, followed a division of his property amongst his children, five sons and two daughters.

The " Homeplace " was given to his sons Ephraim and Atherton. Ephraim had a good house of his own, so he took his share of the property in land, and Atherton went to live in the old homestead. His quarters had been poor enough ; he had not been so successful as his brothers, and had been unable to live as well. It had been a great cross to his wife, Dorcas, who was very high-spirited. She had compared, bitterly, the poverty of her household arrangements, with the abundant comfort of her sisters-in-law.

Now, she seized eagerly at the opportunity of improving her style of living. The old Wales house was quite a pretentious edifice for those times. All the drawback to her delight was, that Grandma should have the southwest fire-room. She wanted to set up her high-posted bedstead, with its enormous feather-bed in that, and have it for her fore-room. Properly, it was the fore-room, being right across the entry from the family sitting-room. There was a tall chest of drawers that would fit in so nicely between the windows, too. Take it altogether, she was chagrined at having to give up the southwest room ; but there was no help for it — there it was in Deacon Wales's will.

Mrs. Dorcas was the youngest of all the sons' wives, as her husband was the latest born. She was quite a girl to some of them. Grandma had never more than half approved of her. Dorcas was high-strung and flighty, she said. She had her doubts about living happily with her. But Atherton was anxious for this division of the property, and he was her youngest darling, so she gave in. She felt lonely, and out of her element, when everything was arranged, she established in the southwest fire-room, and Atherton's family keeping house in the others, though things started pleasantly and peaceably enough.

It occurred to her that her son Samuel might have her own "help," a stout woman, who had worked in her kitchen for many years, and she take in exchange his little bound girl, Ann Ginnins. She had always taken a great fancy to the child. There was a large closet out of the southwest room, where she could sleep, and she could be made very useful, taking steps, and running "arrants" for her.

Mr. Samuel and his wife hesitated a little when this plan was proposed. In spite of the trouble she gave them, they were attached to Ann, and did not like to part with her, and Mrs. Polly was just getting her "larnt" her own ways, as she put it. Privately, she feared Grandma would undo all the good she had done, in teaching Ann to be smart and capable. Finally they gave in, with the understanding that it was not to be considered necessarily a permanent arrangement, and Ann went to live with the old lady.

Mrs. Dorcas did not relish this any more than she did the appropriation of the southwest fire-room. She had never liked Ann very well. Besides she had two little girls of her own, and she fancied Ann rivaled them in Grandma's affection. So, soon after the girl was established in the house, she began to show out in various little ways.

Thirsey, her youngest child, was a mere baby, a round fat dumpling of a thing. She was sweet, and good-natured, and the pet of the whole family. Ann was very fond of playing with her, and tending her, and Mrs. Dorcas began to take advantage of it. The minute Ann was at liberty she was called upon to take care of Thirsey. The constant carrying about such a heavy child soon began to make her shoulders stoop and ache. Then Grandma took up the cudgels. She was smart and high-spirited, but she was a very peaceable old lady on her own account, and fully resolved " to put up with everything from Dorcas, rather than have strife in the family." She was not going to see this helpless little girl imposed on, however. " The little gal ain't goin' to get bent all over, tendin' that heavy baby, Dorcas," she proclaimed. " You can jist make up your mind to it. She didn't come here to do sech work."

So Dorcas had to make up her mind to it.

Ann's principal duties were " scouring the brasses " in Grandma's room, taking steps for her, and spinning her stint every day. Grandma set smaller stints than Mrs. Polly. As time went on, she helped about the cooking.   She and Grandma cooked their own victuals, and ate from a little separate table in the common kitchen.   It was a very large room, and might have accommodated several families, if they could have agreed.   There was a big oven and a roomy fire-place. Good Deacon Wales had probably seen no reason at all why his " beloved wife " should not have her right therein with the greatest peace and concord.

But it soon came to pass that Mrs. Dorcas's pots and kettles were all prepared to hang on the trammels when Grandma's were, and an army of cakes and pies marshaled to go in the oven when Grandma had proposed to do some baking.   Grandma bore it patiently for a long time ; but Ann was with difficulty restrained from freeing her small mind, and her black eyes snapped more dangerously at every new offense.

One morning, Grandma had two loaves of " riz bread," and some election cakes, rising, and was intending to bake them in about an hour, when they should be sufficiently light.   What should Mrs. Dorcas do, but mix up sour milk bread, and some pies with the greatest speed, and fill up the oven, before Grandma's cookery was ready !

Grandma sent Ann out into the kitchen to put the loaves in the oven and lo and behold ! the oven was full.   Ann stood staring for a minute, with a loaf of election cake in her hands ; that and the bread would be ruined if they were not baked immediately, as they

were raised enough.   Mrs. Dorcas had taken Thirsey
and stepped out somewhere, and there was no one in
the kitchen.   Ann set the election cake back on the
table.   Then, with the aid of the tongs, she reached
into the brick oven and took out every one of Mrs.
Dorcas's pies and loaves.   Then she arranged them
deliberately in a pitiful semicircle on the hearth, and
put Grandma's cookery in the oven.

She went back to the southwest room then, and sat
quietly down to her spinning.   Grandma asked if she
had put the things in, and she said "Yes, ma'am,"
meekly.   There was a bright red spot on each of her
dark cheeks.

When Mrs. Dorcas entered the kitchen, carrying
Thirsey wrapped up in an old homespun blanket, she
nearly dropped as her gaze fell on the fire-place and
the hearth.   There sat her bread and pies, in the most
lamentable half-baked, sticky, doughy condition imaginable.   She opened the oven, and peered in.   There
were Grandma's loaves, all a lovely brown.   Out they
came, with a twitch.   Luckily, they were done.   Her
own went in, but they were irretrievable failures.

Of course, quite a commotion came from this.   Dorcas raised her shrill voice pretty high, and Grandma,
though she had been innocent of the whole transaction,
was so blamed that she gave Dorcas a piece of her mind
at last.   Ann surveyed the nice brown loaves, and listened to the talk in secret satisfaction; but she had to

suffer for it afterward. Grandma punished her for the first time, and she discovered that that kind old hand was pretty firm and strong. "No matter what you think or whether you air in the rights on't, or not, a little gal mustn't ever sass her elders," said Grandma.

But if Ann's interference was blamable, it was productive of one good result — the matter came to Mr. Atherton's ears, and he had a stern sense of justice when roused, and a great veneration for his mother. His father's will should be carried out to the letter, he declared; and it was. Grandma baked and boiled in peace, outwardly, at least, after that.

Ann was a great comfort to her; she was outgrowing her wild, mischievous ways, and she was so bright and quick. She promised to be pretty, too. Grandma compared her favorably with her own grandchildren, especially Mrs. Dorcas's eldest daughter Martha, who was nearly Ann's age. "Marthy's a pretty little gal enough," she used to say, "but she ain't got the snap to her that Ann has, though I wouldn't tell Atherton's wife so, for the world."

She promised Ann her gold beads, when she should be done with them, under strict injunctions not to say anything about it till the time came; for the others might feel hard as she wasn't her own flesh and blood. The gold beads were Ann's ideals of beauty and richness, though she did not like to hear Grandma talk about being "done with them." Grandma always wore them around her fair, plump old neck; she had never seen her without her string of beads.

As before said, Ann was now very seldom mischievous enough to make herself serious trouble; but, once in a while, her natural propensities would crop out. When they did, Mrs. Dorcas was exceedingly bitter. Indeed, her dislike of Ann was, at all times, smouldering, and needed only a slight fanning to break out.

One stormy winter day Mrs. Dorcas had been working till dark, making candle-wicks. When she came to get tea, she tied the white fleecy rolls together, a great bundle of them, and hung them up in the cellar-way, over the stair, to be out of the way. They were extra fine wicks, being made of flax for the company candles. "I've got a good job done," said Mrs. Dorcas, surveying them complacently. Her husband had gone to Boston, and was not coming home till the next day, so she had had a nice chance to work at them, without as much interruption as usual.

Ann, going down the cellar stairs, with a lighted candle, after some butter for tea, spied the beautiful rolls swinging overhead. What possessed her to, she could not herself have told — she certainly had no wish to injure Mrs. Dorcas's wicks — but she pinched up a little end of the fluffy flax and touched her candle to it. She thought she would see how that little bit would burn off. She soon found out. The flame caught, and ran like lightning through the whole bundle. There was a great puff of fire and smoke, and poor Mrs. Dorcas's fine candle-wicks were gone. Ann screamed, and sprang downstairs. She barely escaped the whole blaze coming in her face.

"What's that!" shrieked Mrs. Dorcas, rushing to the cellar door. Words cannot describe her feeling when she saw that her nice candle-wicks, the fruit of her day's toil, were burnt up.

If ever there was a wretched culprit that night, Ann was. She had not meant to do wrong, but that, may be, made it worse for her in one way. She had not even gratified malice to sustain her. Grandma blamed her, almost as severely as Mrs. Dorcas. She said she didn't know what would "become of a little gal, that was so keerless," and decreed that she must stay at home from school and work on candle-wicks till Mrs. Dorcas's loss was made good to her. Ann listened ruefully. She was scared and sorry, but that did not seem to help matters any. She did not want any supper, and she went to bed early and cried herself to sleep.

Somewhere about midnight, a strange sound woke her up. She called out to Grandma in alarm. The same sound had awakened her. "Get up, an' light a candle, child," said she; "I'm afeard the baby's sick."

Ann scarcely had the candle lighted, before the door opened, and Mrs. Dorcas appeared in her nightdress.

She was very pale, and trembling all over. "Oh!" she gasped, "it's the baby. Thirsey's got the croup, an' Atherton's away, and there ain't anybody to go for the doctor. Oh, what shall I do, what shall I do!" She fairly wrung her hands.

"Hev you tried the skunk's oil?" asked Grandma eagerly, preparing to get up.

"Yes, I have, I have! It's a good hour since she woke up, an' I've tried everything. It hasn't done any good. I thought I wouldn't call you, if I could help it, but she's worse — only hear her! An' Atherton's away! Oh! what shall I do, what shall I do?"

"Don't take on so, Dorcas," said Grandma, tremulously, but cheeringly. "I'll come right along, an' — why, child, what air you goin' to do?"

Ann had finished dressing herself, and now she was pinning a heavy homespun blanket over her head, as if she were preparing to go out doors.

"I'm going after the doctor for Thirsey," said Ann, her black eyes flashing with determination.

"Oh, will you, will you!" cried Mrs. Dorcas, catching at this new help.

"Hush, Dorcas," said Grandma, sternly. "It's an awful storm out — jist hear the wind blow! It ain't fit fur her to go. Her life's jist as precious as Thirsey's."

Ann said nothing more, but she went into her own

little room with the same determined look in her eyes. There was a door leading from this room into the kitchen. Ann slipped through it hastily, lit a lantern which was hanging beside the kitchen chimney, and was out doors in a minute.

The storm was one of sharp, driving sleet, which struck her face like so many needles. The first blast, as she stepped outside the door, seemed to almost force her back, but her heart did not fail her. The snow was not so very deep, but it was hard walking. There was no pretense of a path. The doctor lived half a mile away, and there was not a house in the whole distance, save the meeting house and schoolhouse. It was very dark. Lucky it was that she had taken the lantern; she could not have found her way without it.

On kept the little slender, erect figure, with the fierce determination in its heart, through the snow and sleet, holding the blanket close over its head, and swinging the feeble lantern bravely.

When she reached the doctor's house, he was gone. He had started for the North Precinct early in the evening, his good wife said; he was called down to Captain Isaac Lovejoy's, the house next the North Precinct Meeting House. She'd been sitting up waiting for him, it was such an awful storm, and such a lonely road. She was worried, but she didn't think he'd start for home that night; she guessed he'd stay at Captain Lovejoy's till morning.

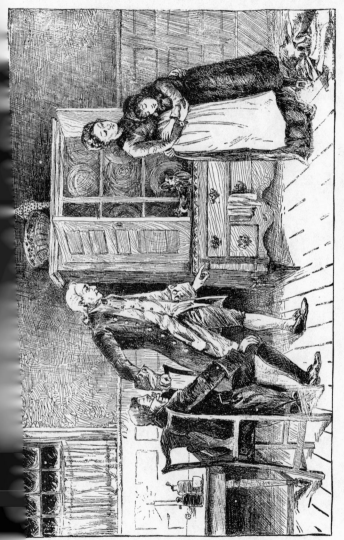

SHE ALMOST FAINTED FROM COLD AND EXHAUSTION.

The doctor's wife, holding her door open, as best she could, in the violent wind, had hardly given this information to the little snow-bedraggled object standing out there in the inky darkness, through which the lantern made a faint circle of light, before she had disappeared.

"She went like a speerit," said the good woman, staring out into the blackness in amazement. She never dreamed of such a thing as Ann's going to the North Precinct after the doctor, but that was what the daring girl had determined to do. She had listened to the doctor's wife in dismay, but with never one doubt as to her own course of proceeding.

Straight along the road to the North Precinct she kept. It would have been an awful journey that night for a strong man. It seemed incredible that a little girl could have the strength or courage to accomplish it. There were four miles to traverse in a black, howling storm, over a pathless road, through forests, with hardly a house by the way.

When she reached Captain Isaac Lovejoy's house, next to the meeting house in the North Precinct of Braintree, stumbling blindly into the warm, lighted kitchen, the captain and the doctor could hardly believe their senses. She told the doctor about Thirsey; then she almost fainted from cold and exhaustion.

Good-wife Lovejoy laid her on the settee, and brewed her some hot herb tea. She almost forgot her own sick little girl, for a few minutes, in trying to restore this brave child who had come from the South Precinct in this dreadful storm to save little Thirsey Wales's life.

When Ann came to herself a little, her first question was, if the doctor were ready to go.

"He's gone," said Mrs. Lovejoy, cheeringly.

Ann felt disappointed. She had thought she was going back with him. But that would have been impossible. She could not have stood the journey for the second time that night, even on horseback behind the doctor, as she had planned.

She drank a second bowlful of herb tea, and went to bed with a hot stone at her feet, and a great many blankets and coverlids over her.

The next morning, Captain Lovejoy carried her home. He had a rough wood sled, and she rode on that, on an old quilt; it was easier than horseback, and she was pretty lame and tired.

Mrs. Dorcas saw her coming and opened the door. When Ann came up on the stoop, she just threw her arms around her and kissed her.

"You needn't make the candle-wicks," said she. "It's no matter about them at all. Thirsey's better this morning, an' I guess you saved her life."

Grandma was fairly bursting with pride and delight in her little gal's brave feat, now that she saw her safe. She untied the gold beads on her neck, and fastened them around Ann's. "There," said she, "you may wear them to school to-day, if you'll be keerful."

That day, with the gold beads by way of celebration, began a new era in Ann's life. There was no more secret animosity between her and Mrs. Dorcas. The doctor had come that night in the very nick of time. Thirsey was almost dying. Her mother was fully convinced that Ann had saved her life, and she never forgot it. She was a woman of strong feelings, who never did things by halves, and she not only treated Ann with kindness, but she seemed to smother her grudge against Grandma for robbing her of the south-west fire-room.

THE ADOPTED DAUGHTER.

THE Inventory of the Estate of Samuel Wales Late of Braintree, Taken by the Subscribers, March the 14th, 1761.

His Purse in Cash	£11–15–01
His apparrel	. 10–11–00
His watch	. 2–13–04
The Best Bed with two Coverlids, three sheets, two underbeds, two Bolsters, two pillows, Bedstead rope	£6
One mill Blanket, two Phlauel sheets, 12 toe Sheets	£ 3– 4– 8
Eleven Towels & table Cloth	. 0–15– 0
a pair of mittens & pr. of Gloves	. 0– 2– 0
a neck Handkerchief & neckband	. 0– 4– 0
an ovel Tabel — Two other Tabels . . .	. 1–12– 0
A Chist with Draws	. 2– 8– 0
Another Low Chist with Draws & three other Chists	. 1–10– 0
Six best Chears and a great chear	. 1– 6– 0
a warming pan — Two Brass Kittles . . .	. 1– 5– 0
a Small Looking Glass, five Pewter Basons . .	. 0– 7– 8
fifteen other Chears ˙	. 0–15– 0
fire arms, Sword & bayonet	. 1– 4– 0
Six Porringers, four platters, Two Pewter Pots .	£ 1– 0– 4
auger Chisel, Gimlet, a Bible & other Books . .	. 0–15– 4
A chese press, great spinning-wheel, & spindle .	. 0– 9– 0

a smith's anvil	.	.	.	.	.	.	.	.£ 3–12– 0
the Pillion	.	.	.	.	.	.	.	. 0– 8– 0
a Bleu Jacket .	.	.	.	.	.	.	.	. 0– 0– 3

AARON WHITCOMB.
SILAS WHITE.

The foregoing is only a small portion of the original inventory of Samuel Wales's estate. He was an exceedingly well-to-do man for these times. He had a good many acres of rich pasture and woodland, and considerable live stock. Then his home was larger and more comfortable than was usual then; and his stock of household utensils plentiful.

He died three years after Ann Ginnins went to live with Grandma, when she was about thirteen years old. Grandma spared her to Mrs. Polly for a few weeks after the funeral; there was a great deal to be done, and she needed some extra help. And, after all, Ann was legally bound to her, and her lawful servant.

So the day after good Samuel Wales was laid away in the little Braintree burying-ground, Ann returned to her old quarters for a little while. She did not really want to go; but she did not object to the plan at all. She was sincerely sorry for poor Mrs. Polly, and wanted to help her, if she could. She mourned, herself, for Mr. Samuel. He had always been very kind to her.

Mrs. Polly had for company, besides Ann, Nabby Porter, Grandma's old hired woman whom she had made over to her, and a young man who had been serving as apprentice to Mr. Samuel. His name was Phineas Adams. He was very shy and silent, but a good workman.

Samuel Wales left a will bequeathing everything to his widow; that was solemnly read in the fore-room one afternoon; then th₊ inventory had to be taken. That, on account of the amount of property, was quite an undertaking; but it was carried out with the greatest formality and precision.

For several days, Mr. Aaron Whitcomb and Mr. Silas White were stalking majestically about the premises, with note-books and pens. Aaron Whitcomb was a grave, portly old man, with a large head of white hair. Silas White was little and wiry and fussy. He monopolized the greater part of the business, although he was not half as well fitted for it as his companion.

They pried into everything with religious exactitude. Mrs. Polly watched them with beseeming awe and deference, but it was a great trial to her, and she grew very nervous over it. It seemed dreadful to have all her husband's little personal effects, down to his neckband and mittens, handled over, and their worth in shillings and pence calculated. She had a price fixed on them already in higher currency.

Ann found her crying one afternoon sitting on the kitchen settle, with her apron over her head. When she saw the little girl's pitying look, she poured out her trouble to her.

" They've just been valuing his mittens and gloves," said she, sobbing, " at two-and-sixpence. I shall be thankful when they are through."

" Are there any more of his things ? " asked Ann, her black eyes flashing, with the tears in them.

" I think they've seen about all. There's his blue jacket he used to milk in, a-hanging behind the shed door — I guess they haven't valued that yet."

" I think it's a shame ! " quoth Ann. " I don't believe there's any need of so much law."

" Hush, child ! You mustn't set yourself up against the judgment of your elders. Such things have to be done."

Ann said no more, but the indignant sparkle did not fade out of her eyes at all. She watched her opportunity, and took down Mr. Wales's old blue jacket from its peg behind the shed door, ran with it upstairs, and hid it in her own room behind the bed. " There," said she, " Mrs. Wales sha'n't cry over that ! "

That night, at tea time, the work of taking the inventory was complete. Mr. Whitcomb and Mr. White walked away with their long lists, satisfied that they had done their duty according to the law. Every article of Samuel Wales's property, from a warming pan to a chest of drawers, was set down, with the sole exception of that old blue jacket, which Ann had hidden.

She felt complacent over it at first ; then she began to be uneasy.

" Nabby," said she confidentially to the old servant woman, when they were washing the pewter plates together after supper, " what would they do if anybody shouldn't let them set down all the things — if they hid some of 'em away, I mean ? "

" They'd make a dretful time on't," said Nabby impressively. She was a large, stern-looking old woman. " They air dretful perticklar 'bout these things. They hev to be."

Ann was scared when she heard that. When the dishes were done, she sat down on the settle and thought it over, and made up her mind what to do.

The next morning, in the frosty dawning, before the rest of the family were up, a slim, erect little figure could have been seen speeding across lots toward Mr. Silas White's. She had the old blue jacket tucked under her arm. When she reached the house, she spied Mr. White just coming out of the back door with a milking pail. He carried a lantern, too, for it was hardly light.

He stopped and stared when Ann ran up to him.

" Mr. White," said she, all breathless, " here's — something — I guess yer didn't see yesterday."

Mr. White set down the milk pail, took the blue

jacket which she handed him, and scrutinized it sharply
by the light of the lantern.

"I guess we didn't see it," said he finally. "I will
put it down — it's worth about three pence, I judge.
Where " —

"Silas, Silas!" called a shrill voice from the house.
Silas White dropped the jacket and trotted briskly in,
his lantern bobbing agitatedly. He never delayed a
moment when his wife called; important and tyranni-
cal as the little man was abroad, he had his own tyrant
at home.

Ann did not wait for him to return; she snatched
up the blue jacket and fled home, leaping like a little
deer over the hoary fields. She hung up the precious
old jacket behind the shed door again, and no one ever
knew the whole story of its entrance in the inventory.
If she had been questioned, she would have told the
truth boldly, though. But Samuel Wales's Inventory
had for its last item that blue jacket, spelled after Silas
White's own individual method, as was many another
word in the long list. Silas White consulted his own
taste with respect to capital letters too.

After a few weeks, Grandma said she must have Ann
again; and back she went. Grandma was very feeble
lately, and everybody humored her. Mrs. Polly was
sorry to have the little girl leave her. She said it was
wonderful how much she had improved. But she
would not have admitted that the improvement was

owing to the different influence she had been under; she said Ann had outgrown her mischievous ways.

Grandma did not live very long after this, however. Mrs. Polly had her bound girl at her own disposal in a year's time. Poor Ann was sorrowful enough for a long while after Grandma's death. She wore the beloved gold beads round her neck, and a sad ache in her heart. The dear old woman had taken the beads off her neck with her own hands and given them to Ann before she died, that there might be no mistake about it.

Mrs. Polly said she was glad Ann had them. " You might jist as well have 'em as Dorcas's girl," said she ; " she set enough sight more by you."

Ann could not help growing cheerful again, after a while. Affairs in Mrs. Polly's house were much brighter for her, in some ways, than they had ever been before.

Either the hot iron of affliction had smoothed some of the puckers out of her mistress's disposition, or she was growing, naturally, less sharp and dictatorial. Any way, she was becoming as gentle and loving with Ann as it was in her nature to be, and Ann, following her impulsive temper, returned all the affection with vigor, and never bestowed a thought on past unpleasantness.

For the next two years, Ann's position in the family grew to be more and more that of a daughter. If it had not been for the indentures, lying serenely in that tall wooden desk, she would almost have forgotten, herself, that she was a bound girl.

One spring afternoon, when Ann was about sixteen years old, her mistress called her solemnly into the fore-room. " Ann," said she, "come here, I want to speak to you."

Nabby stared wonderingly; and Ann, as she obeyed, felt awed. There was something unusual in her mistress's tone.

Standing there in the fore-room, in the august company of the best bed, with its high posts and flowered-chintz curtains, the best chest of drawers, and the best chairs, Ann listened to what Mrs. Polly had to tell her. It was a plan which almost took her breath away; for it was this: Mrs. Polly proposed to adopt her, and change her name to Wales. She would be no longer Ann Ginnins, and a bound girl; but Ann Wales, and a daughter in her mother's home.

Ann dropped into one of the best chairs, and sat there, her little dark face very pale. "Should I have the — papers ? " she gasped at length.

" Your papers ? Yes, child, you can have them."

" I don't want them," cried Ann, " never ! I want them to stay just where they are, till my time is out. If I am adopted, I don't want the papers ! "

Mrs. Polly stared. She had never known how Ann had taken the indentures with her on her run-away trip years ago; but now Ann told her the whole story. In her gratitude to her mistress, and her contrition, she had to.

It was so long ago in Ann's childhood, it did not seem so very dreadful to Mrs. Polly, probably. But Ann insisted on the indentures remaining in the desk, even after the papers of adoption were made out, and she had become "Ann Wales." It seemed to go a little way toward satisfying her conscience. This adoption meant a good deal to Ann; for besides a legal home, and a mother, it secured to her a right in a comfortable property in the future. Mrs. Polly Wales was considered very well off. She was a smart business-woman, and knew how to take care of her property too. She still hired Phineas Adams to carry on the blacksmith's business, and kept her farm-work running just as her husband had. Neither she nor Ann were afraid of work, and Ann Wales used to milk the cows, and escort them to and from pasture, as faithfully as Ann Ginnins.

It was along in springtime when Ann was adopted, and Mrs. Polly fulfilled her part of the contract in the indentures by getting the Sunday suit therein spoken of.

They often rode on horseback to meeting, but they usually walked on the fine Sundays in spring. Ann had probably never been so happy in her life as she was walking by Mrs. Polly's side to meeting that first Sunday after her adoption. Most of the way was

through the woods ; the tender light green boughs met
over their heads ; the violets and anemones were
springing beside their path. There were green buds
and white blossoms all around ; the sky showed blue
between the waving branches, and the birds were
singing.

Ann in her pretty petticoat of rose-colored stuff,
stepping daintily over the young grass and the flowers,
looked and felt like a part of it all. Her dark cheeks
had a beautiful red glow on them ; her black eyes shone.
She was as straight and graceful and stately as an
Indian.

"She's as handsome as a picture," thought Mrs.
Polly in her secret heart. A good many people said
that Ann resembled Mrs. Polly in her youth, and that
may have added force to her admiration.

Her new gown was very fine for those days ; but
fine as she was, and adopted daughter though she was,
Ann did not omit her thrifty ways for once. This
identical morning Mrs. Polly and she carried their best
shoes under their arms, and wore their old ones, till
within a short distance from the meeting-house. Then
the old shoes were tucked away under a stone wall for
safety, and the best ones put on. Stone walls, very
likely, sheltered a good many well-worn little shoes, of
a Puritan Sabbath, that their prudent owners might
appear in the House of God trimly shod. Ah ! these
beautiful, new, peaked-toed, high-heeled shoes of Ann's

— what would she have said to walking in them all the way to meeting!

If that Sunday was an eventful one to Ann Wales, so was the week following. The next Tuesday, right after dinner, she was up in a little unfinished chamber over the kitchen, where they did such work when the weather permitted, carding wool. All at once, she heard voices down below. They had a strange inflection, which gave her warning at once. She dropped her work and listened. "What is the matter?" thought she.

Then there was a heavy tramp on the stairs, and Captain Abraham French stood in the door, his stern weather-beaten face white and set. Mrs. Polly followed him, looking very pale and excited.

"When did you see anything of our Hannah?" asked Captain French, controlling as best he could the tremor in his resolute voice.

Ann rose, gathering up her big blue apron, cards, wool and all. "Oh," she cried, "not since last Sabbath, at meeting! What is it?"

"She's lost," answered Captain French. "She started to go up to her Aunt Sarah's Monday forenoon; and Enos has just been down, and they haven't seen anything of her." Poor Captain French gave a deep groan.

Then they all went down into the kitchen together, talking and lamenting. And then, Captain French was galloping away on his gray horse to call assistance, and Ann was flying away over the fields, blue apron, cards, wool and all.

" O, Ann ! " Mrs. Polly cried after, " where are you going ? "

" I'm going — to find — Hannah ! " Ann shouted back, in a shrill, desperate voice, and kept on.

She had no definite notion as to where she was going ; she had only one thought — Hannah French, her darling, tender, little Hannah French, her friend whom she loved better than a sister, was lost.

A good three miles from the Wales home was a large tract of rough land, half-swamp, known as " Bear Swamp." There was an opinion, more or less correct, that bears might be found there. Some had been shot in that vicinity. Why Ann turned her footsteps in that direction, she could not have told herself. Possibly the vague impression of conversations she and Hannah had had, lingering in her mind, had something to do with it. Many a time the two little girls had remarked to each other with a shudder, " How awful it would be to get lost in Bear Swamp."

Any way, Ann went straight there, through pasture and woodland, over ditches and stone walls. She knew every step of the way for a long distance. When she gradually got into the unfamiliar wilderness of the swamp, a thought struck her — suppose she got lost too ! It would be easy enough — the unbroken forest stretched for miles in some directions.   She would not find a living thing but Indians, and, maybe, wild beasts, the whole distance.

If she should get lost she would not find Hannah, and the people would have to hunt for her too.   But Ann had quick wits for an emergency.   She had actually carried those cards, with a big wad of wool between them all the time, in her gathered-up apron.   Now she began picking off little bits of wool and marking her way with them, sticking them on the trees and bushes. Every few feet a fluffy scrap of wool showed the road Ann had gone.

But poor Ann went on, farther and farther — and no sign of Hannah.   She kept calling her from time to time, hallooing at the top of her shrill sweet voice : " Hannah ! Hannah ! Hannah Fre-nch ! "

But never a response got the dauntless little girl, slipping almost up to her knees sometimes, in black swamp-mud ; and sometimes stumbling painfully over tree-stumps, and through tangled undergrowth.

" I'll go till my wool gives out," said Ann Wales ; then she used it more sparingly.

But it was almost gone before she thought she heard in the distance a faint little cry in response to her call : " Hannah ! Hannah Fre-nch ! "   She called again and listened.   Yes ; she certainly did hear a little cry off toward the west.   Calling from time to time, she went as nearly as she could in that direction.   The pitiful answering cry grew louder and nearer; finally Ann could distinguish Hannah's voice.

Wild with joy, she came, at last, upon her sitting on a fallen hemlock-tree, her pretty face pale, and her sweet blue eyes strained with terror.

" O, Hannah!" "O, Ann!"

" How did you ever get here, Hannah?"

" I — started for aunt Sarah's — that morning," explained Hannah, between sobs. "And — I got frightened in the woods, about a mile from father's. I saw something ahead I thought was a bear. A great black thing! Then I ran — and, somehow, the first thing I knew, I was lost. I walked and walked, and it seems to me I kept coming right back to the same place. Finally I sat down here, and staid; I thought it was all the way for me to be found."

" O, Hannah! what did you do last night?"

" I staid somewhere, under some pine-trees," replied Hannah, with a shudder; "and I kept hearing things — O, Ann!"

Ann hugged her sympathizingly. "I guess I wouldn't have slept much if I had known," said she. "O, Hannah, you haven't had anything to eat! ain't you starved?"

Hannah laughed faintly. "I ate up two whole pumpkin pies I was carrying to aunt Sarah," said she.

" Oh! how lucky it was you had them."

" Yes; mother called me back to get them, after I

started. They were some new ones, made with cream, and she thought aunt Sarah would like them."

Pretty soon they started. It was hard work, for the way was very rough, and poor Hannah weak. But Ann had a good deal of strength in her lithe young frame, and she half-carried Hannah over the worst places. Still both of the girls were pretty well spent when they came to the last of the bits of wool on the border of Bear Swamp. However, they kept on a little farther; then they had to stop and rest. "I know where I am now," said Hannah, with a sigh of delight; "but I don't think I can walk another step." She was, in fact, almost exhausted.

Ann looked at her thoughtfully. She hardly knew what to do. She could not carry Hannah herself — indeed, her own strength began to fail; and she did not want to leave her to go for assistance.

All of a sudden, she jumped up. "You stay just where you are a few minutes, Hannah," said she. "I'm going somewhere. I'll be back soon." Ann was laughing.

Hannah looked up at her pitifully: "O Ann, don't go!"

"I'm coming right back, and it is the only way. You must get home. Only think how your father and mother are worrying!"

Hannah said no more after that mention of her parents, and Ann started.

A CONVEYANCE IS FOUND.

She was not gone long. When she came in sight she was laughing, and Hannah, weak as she was, laughed, too. Ann had torn her blue apron into strips, and tied it together for a rope, and by it she was leading a red cow.

Hannah knew the cow, and knew at once what the plan was. "O, Ann! you mean for me to ride Betty?"

"Of course I do. I just happened to think our cows were in the pasture, down below here. And we've ridden Betty, lots of times, when we were children, and she's just as gentle now. Whoa, Betty, good cow."

It was very hard work to get Hannah on to the broad back of her novel steed, but it was finally accomplished. Betty had been a perfect pet from a calf, and was exceedingly gentle. She started off soberly across the fields, with Hannah sitting on her back, and Ann leading her by her blue rope.

It was a funny cavalcade for Captain Abraham French and a score of anxious men to meet, when they were nearly in sight of home; but they were too overjoyed to see much fun in it.

Hannah rode the rest of the way with her father, on his gray horse; and Ann walked joyfully by her side, leading the cow.

Captain French and his friends had, in fact, just started to search Bear Swamp, well armed with lanterns, for night was coming on.

It was dark when they got home. Mrs. French was not much more delighted to see her beloved daughter Hannah safe again, than Mrs. Polly was to see Ann.

She listened admiringly to the story Ann told.

" Nobody but you would have thought of the wool or of the cow," said she.

" I do declare," cried Ann, at the mention of the wool, " I have lost the cards ! "

" Never mind the cards ! " said Mrs. Polly.

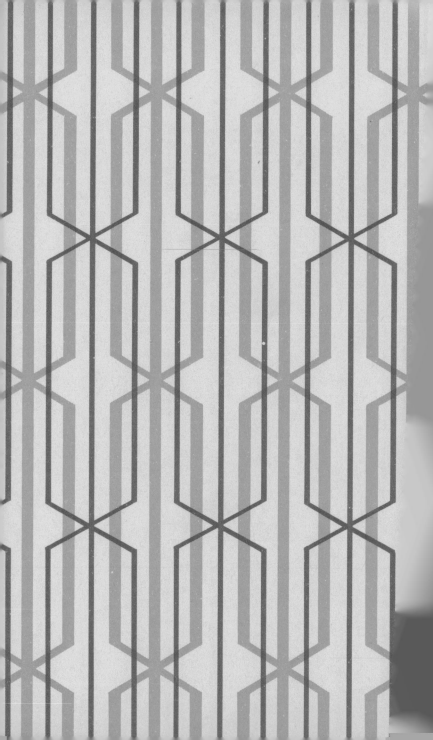